I0678729

Lady of the Lake and Other Short Stories

A Collection of Short Stories
By
Richard Golden

Published by New Generation Publishing in 2014

Copyright © Richard Golden 2014

First Edition

The author asserts the moral right under the Copyright, Designs and Patents Act 1988 to be identified as the author of this work.

All Rights reserved. No part of this publication may be reproduced, stored in a retrieval system or transmitted, in any form or by any means without the prior consent of the author, nor be otherwise circulated in any form of binding or cover other than that which it is published and without a similar condition being imposed on the subsequent purchaser.

www.newgeneration-publishing.com

 New Generation **Publishing**

For my wife, Mary and children,
Catherine, Clare and John

CONTENTS

Lady of the Lake

The engine of the little boat chugged away in the evening light as it made its way towards the shore. The figure of Nora Doran grew larger and larger. The place was peaceful now - not at all like last week.

She knew all the time they would never find the body of the Englishman.

Nora Doran loved Lough Gara and felt part of it. Had she not been bred, born and starved by its waters? Here she would die too and be buried above there in the graveyard at Cloonloo in the shelter of the yew trees. There, she would be able to hear the soft sounds of the waves gently lapping the shore.

Generations of her family were buried there. Gravestones, old and new, kept watch on the ruins of an earlier church. Only the stone wall separated this quiet spot from the lake. In the distance the remains of ancient crannogs bore witness to another time and another people. Yet, you could almost sense their presence in this enchanting and beautiful place.

Nora knew only too well the dangers of the lake especially for the unsuspecting visitor. She lost her own father when still a slip of a young girl. His body was not found for nine days. That was a long time ago but the memory was still vivid. There were others too.

The members of the Garda diving team had packed away their equipment and departed to some other job. So too had all the reporters - local and national press, radio and television. Flynn's Public House would notice the difference. Michael Richard Gillighan would have to buy his own drinks from now on. Nora Doran had watched it all from her small kitchen window. Still, Lough Gara kept its morbid secret.

The papers said he had been on a fishing trip from England. Some of the best fishing waters in Ireland were to be found in this part of the country. He kept himself very much to himself. Occasionally, at night, he would sit in the corner of Flynn's sipping a pint of Guinness and just listening to the banter of country folk. Sometimes he would ask the local people questions about this and that. For a stranger he had a curious interest in the goings on of the locality.

The wind was quite fresh now and Nora scarcely heard Michael Richard – or as he was better known, Mickey Dick – calling.

"Mrs Doran! Mrs Doran! Can you hear me?"

Mickey Dick was waving his old cloth cap frantically in the air.

"Yoo ...hoo, ... Yoo hoo!" he shouted.

At last she noticed his efforts to attract her attention and acknowledged.

"What can he want?" she wondered, at the same time easing up on the throttle and steering the boat towards the small landing.

Each day Nora Doran made the trip to the island. The land was good with an easily accessible supply of drinking water. You never knew when a beast might get into difficulty. This was part of the routine and ritual of her hard life for years now. If she had married a half-decent sort of man instead of Danjo perhaps things might have been different. Nora thought about her husband and the wasted life he had – him and his politics. No trouble for him to stay up half the night with his cronies putting the old country right when he spent the day in bed. Nora was feeling angry. These were not the kind of thoughts she wished to dwell upon.

Nora Doran loved the lake, which dominated her whole existence. You couldn't avoid it because it was always there - summer and winter. Each season brought its own changes. She remembered the hard winters when it would completely freeze over. In the really severe years they would cart loads of turf across the frozen lake. A sledgehammer would not break through it. Then the thaw would come. The cracking and groaning of the ice in the watery winter sun could be heard a mile away.

It was a popular place in the summer too. She smiled to herself when she recalled the time the Bishop's boat ran aground on some rocks. Didn't her poor father, God rest him, wade out in the water to rescue him and carry him to safety on his back.

"I've got news for you, Mrs Doran," yelled Mickey Dick.

"Well it must be important news, surely, and the way you've been going on."

The boat came to rest in its usual place at the end of the landing.

"Here, you old fool, grab the rope and tie her up." demanded Nora.

"I think that ould engine has nearly had it, Mrs Doran."

"A bit like myself, it is." added Nora.

She gave a hearty laugh at the same time struggling to keep her balance. The wind was much stronger now.

"Can I give you a hand Mrs Doran?"

"Indeed you will not, it's not helpless I

am you know.   Anyway, what's all the excitement about?"

"I've got some important news for you Mrs Doran." said Mickey Dick.

She detected the rather serious tone in his voice now.

"There's seldom much news around these parts," she thought to herself, "only bad news."

"They've been asking questions again, Nora," he whispered at the same time glancing around in case anyone was listening.

There was no need to worry. Only the sound of the wind blowing through the leaves of the trees in the graveyard could be heard and the lapping of the waves below. Nora was serious too - the carefree expression had left her face.

"And who's been asking the questions, Mickey Dick?"

"Them detective fellows down from the City."

"They should let the dead rest in peace."

"What are we going to do Nora...what are we going to do?"

Nora paused for a while obviously deep in thought. Heaven knows she hadn't wanted all this trouble. This was a quiet place or was it, she wondered. People just wanted to be left alone to get on with their lives.

The Guards had spent two weeks searching for the body. She knew all the time that search was in vain.

"Why did he have to come around these parts at all?" she thought.

"What did you tell them Mickey Dick?"

"I told them nothing so I didn't."

"Are you sure about that now?"

"Swear to God I *am* Nora. Sure I'm no squealer."

"Good, good - just keep calm and everything will be alright."

"By God I hope you're right, Nora."

"But we're going to have to do something quickly."

"Do something...and what are we going to do?"

"I don't know but we cannot leave things the way they are," added Nora as they started to walk up the road from the lake.

Danjo woke to hear the voices of Nora and Mickey Dick in the kitchen. The effects of the day's quota of alcohol were beginning to wear off by now. While drinking a cup of Nora's strong tea he listened to Mickey Dick repeating his story.

"We've got to move fast, Danjo," interrupted Nora, impatiently, "It can't wait any longer."

"Ah I know that alright."

"It must be tonight - there's a good moon."

"We'll never get away with it, it's too risky," added Mickey.

"Now listen to me" said Nora "this is the plan...."

Mickey Dick and Danjo worked away quietly in the moonlight while Nora kept watch from behind one of the tall yew trees. She knew it was only a matter of days - hours, perhaps - before they would turn their attention to Cloonloo Graveyard. Now, they had to move fast. Maybe it had been a bad idea after all hiding the poor unfortunate man's body here. Certainly, he was not going to get any rest!

9

Mickey Dick and Danjo were hidden from view by the walls of the old ruined church little of which remained standing now. The two shadowy figures worked relentlessly removing the soft soil.

"This was no way for a man to end his days," thought Nora, as she listened to the steady rhythm of the spades digging away. He did not have to die in this lonesome place. Those who sent him should have known better. You had to live in these parts to know what went on and then you minded your own business. It was no place for prying strangers from across the water.

Life in this part of the country had always been hard. Years spent toiling to make a living was etched on the faces of the people who lived here. Few houses remained now thanks to the ravages of immigration and the drift from the land. Today, the sound of children's laughter was seldom heard. Only the barking of a dog or a fox broke the silence of the night.

The sight of long abandoned homes with their caved in roofs and tattered curtains made Nora sad. For her they held poignant memories - weddings and wake houses, births and deaths...The stranger would not have the privilege of a decent funeral amongst friends. Somewhere, a wife and children, perhaps, will grieve.

The two men struggled as they lifted the body over the stonewall and eased it gently onto the grass beyond. A man is treated with more respect and dignity in death than life. Yet, there was damn all dignity in this sordid affair. In the shelter of the Birch trees they carried his body to the lakeshore.

"I'll grab the shoulders and you take the legs, Mickey Dick," said Danjo, heart pounding and out of breath.

Slowly, the wet muddy body was lifted into the tiny boat, which was kept steady by Nora.

"Be careful there now with the poor man." said Nora.

She quickly realised the irony of those words.

"Now with a couple of concrete blocks for company at the bottom of the lake he won't be troubling us any more," said Danjo.

"How right you are, Danjo - they'll not be bothered dragging Lough Gara again," replied Mickey Dick, suddenly sounding quite brave and pleased with himself.

"He'll not be found at those depths. God rest his soul," added Nora.

She watched as they disappeared into the darkness of the night. Then Nora Doran turned for home. Walking up the road her thoughts were suddenly shattered by the sound of the powerful explosion that illuminated the lake waters.

Once again, death had cast its dark shadow over the lake.

A Shortcut to Rathbeg

The Fox Frayne ended his night of card playing as it had begun - on a winning streak. He was no mean card player by any man's standard but tonight he surprised himself, not to mention the others. However, he knew only too well that his success was not entirely due to skill, or good luck, for that matter.

The church clock struck midnight as he donned his heavy overcoat and old battered cap and set out for home. He did not forget to put his favorite pack of cards in his pocket. It was a bitterly cold and windy night as he took the short cut across the fields and through the woods.

"I'll be home and tucked up in me bed in no time at all" he thought. The clouds raced across the moonlit sky casting eerie shadows over the fields with their grey stone walls. He wrapped his scarf tightly around his neck and put his head down against the biting east wind.

Fox Frayne or, as he was usually called, 'The Fox", hadn't gone very far when he heard the unmistakable sound of music carried on the wind. This was a great part of the country for good lively traditional music. Yet, somehow, this music sounded different to his ears and it seemed to be getting louder and louder.

"That's the sweetest music I've ever heard," he said to himself.

Carefully, he picked his steps along the stone wall trying to find out where the music was coming from. It was as if some strange force, which he did not understand, was drawing him towards it. By now he had wandered some distance from his original path without realising it. He peeped over the stone wall and it was then that he saw the strangest sight of his life. For there in the middle of the field was a troop of tiny little men and women and them no taller than the length of your arm. Each one was playing an instrument of some kind - fiddles and flutes, pipes and piccolos. There was a drummer too. They marched around a tall solitary Whitethorn tree playing, dancing and singing as they went:

   Hiddle de Hi
   Hiddle de Ho!
   Hail and rain
   Frost and snow.
   Catch Foxy Frayne
   and don't let him go,
   Hiddle de Hi
   Hiddle de Ho!

The Fox froze as he surveyed this incredible scene making sure, of course, that he was not seen. It was then that it dawned upon him that he was lost.

"God Blast it! Which way at all is it to Rathbeg?" he muttered, setting off once more and feeling pleased that at least the small people had not noticed him. Still, their haunting song sent a chill right down his spine.

The wind was really blowing now and he had forgotten about his successful night's card playing until he felt the cards in his pocket. Desperately, he searched for some familiar landmark, which would point him in the right direction for home. He came to a stile in a stone wall. There, sitting on the stile and looking quite ferocious in the darkness, was the biggest black cat you have ever seen. As Fox Frayne approached the cat, it made no attempt to move.

"Shush!" says he "Get out of me way, isn't it a great hurry I'm in this night."

"Indeed then I will not," said the cat.

Frayne was absolutely flabbergasted. Now that drop of poteen, which Mrs. Flanagan kept for purely medicinal reasons, was powerful stuff alright but the sight of little people dancing around a tree in the middle of the night and now a talking cat was a bit too much for him.

"Now, if you take my advice," says the cat "you'll turn right here and follow the stream and don't stop whatever happens until you reach Rathbeg."

The Fox didn't argue but set off at a quick pace following the course of the little river. He felt terror in his heart of a kind he had never known before that night. He walked and walked but still every place seemed strange. Battling against the wind, which was now much stronger, he did not stop even to draw his breath. If he did not reach home soon he knew he would be in trouble.

He thought about the music of the little people which had lured him from his familiar path and their haunting song. The words spoken by the black cat too rang in his ears.

"Don't stop whatever happens until you reach Rathbeg." The storm was now raging and he could scarcely get his breath. It was becoming dangerous too. A large tree crashed to the ground narrowly missing him. He was now becoming exhausted and knew he couldn't keep going for much longer.

"If only there was some place to shelter." he wished.

It was then he saw in the distance a neatly thatched and whitewashed cottage. There was light shining through the small kitchen window.

"I'll enquire here for directions," he thought to himself.

He was beginning to feel warmer and more relaxed as he approached the front door of the house.

"A little rest and maybe a hot cup of strong tea would do me good." he thought.

Twice he knocked on the door and waited. There was no answer. Looking at his watch, he saw that it was now four o'clock in the morning. Was it really as late as that, he wondered?

"I must have walked miles - no wonder me poor legs are killing me," he muttered to himself, at the same time knocking on the door once more. Despite the howling of the wind he could hear voices coming from inside. He listened more intently now, as he waited for someone to answer.

"This one is mine, I tell you," said a rather gruff sounding voice.

"It is not," answered another voice quite emphatically.

"Well we shall see then, won't we?" said the gruff voice.

"That we will indeed," replied the other.

Still no one came to the door. The Fox tried the latch and gently opened the door and entered.

Inside there were two men seated at a table card playing. A large turf fire burned. He noticed that one of the men was tall with dark clothes and an upturned collar. He could not see his face clearly as his back was turned towards him. The second man was easier to see in the light of the hurricane lamp, which hung from the rafters and swung to and fro in the draught.

He noticed that the second man was dressed in priests' clothing of the type worn in the last century. Not a single word was spoken as the two men continued to play cards apparently unaware of his presence. The sight of an empty chair at the table between the two men made him feel uneasy.

"Had someone just left or perhaps they are expecting someone," he wondered, feeling decidedly nervous.

"Come up here and take a seat Frayne," said the tall man with the upturned collar and gruff voice. The priest smiled and beckoned to him to be seated. The Fox was relieved to be inside and out of the storm, which seemed to shake the whole house with enormous strength.

"I'm glad you've come," said the one with the gruff voice, "I've waited a long time for you."

Outside, a cat gave a pitiful cry and Frayne felt bewildered.

"Where am I? Can ... Can you tell me how to get to Rathbeg?" he asked nervously.

His heart was beating so loud he wondered if they could hear it. The one with the gruff voice laughed - a loud menacing laugh that pierced his ears.

"There is only one place you are going," said the gruff one, "I have bet your soul on this game of cards and tonight you'll be mine"

Again, outside the cat gave another loud

wail. The Fox Frayne wished he had not cheated at cards that night.

With that, the priest played a card and at the same time a cock crowed in the yard. There was a mighty flash and a loud bang as the place filled with smoke.

He woke up, as dawn broke, by the side of a ditch a short distance from Rathbeg and all that remained was the smell of sulphur in the air. From that day until the day he died, The Fox Frayne never played a game of cards again.

Kate the Bush

I followed my father's heavy footsteps up the narrow winding staircase, which lead to a door marked "Burke and McGurk, Solicitors and Commissioners of Oaths"

"Come in.", called an elderly male voice.

My father slowly turned the brass knob and opened the door. I followed.

"Ah Mr.Mulhare, how nice to see you".

"It's about the letter..."

"Yes, yes - the late Mary Kate Quinn," interrupted Mr.McGurk.

"I'll just get the papers."

We had buried 'Kate the Bush' a few days earlier. The door creaked and moaned as it closed behind the solicitor. The office was untidy with files piled high on an old table in the centre, which acted as a desk. The place was dull and musty. I sensed the nervous anticipation, which made Dad's face look strained and felt uncomfortable. Through the curtained window I watched the leaves dance in the gentle whirlwind outside. The ticking of the clock on the wall broke the silence, releasing forgotten memories...

There is something unnerving about the ticking of a clock. I recalled the ticking of Mary Kate's old clock. Then I remembered my father's stern warnings about "that old hag, Kate the Bush", and all the stories I had heard about her.

She was a woman in her late fifties when we met that October morning. Mary Kate lived on a few acres of rushy land. The small whitewashed cottage lay in the shadows of the big Ash trees where the road bent sharply to the left. It looked out on the vast expanse of bog land with its many shades of brown and the silvery lake beyond. She wore a dirty patterned apron with black stockings and thick brogues. Mary Kate would hide behind a tree peeping at passersby and we called her "Kate the Bush".

Mary Kate had achieved a degree of notoriety in her lifetime. With the passing years the old lady had become more crabbed. The very mention of her name was enough to send a shiver up my spine.

If only half the stories told were to be believed she was the nearest thing to a witch you were ever likely to find in the West of Ireland. Indeed, I was convinced she was a witch. Some of the neighbours said she could put a powerful curse on you if she took a dislike.

"Be God a Christ, I'll throttle him," said Mary Kate one day when Grabber Gallagher had an eye on her bit of land.

With her it was very much a case of a few prayers interspersed with a litany of curses that would make Old Nick himself blush. My father would often talk about the time she caught a fox attacking her hens and strangled it with her bare hands. Kate the Bush then cut out the unfortunate creature's tongue and took it to the Garda Barracks to collect her five-shilling bounty.

Then there was the time she turned on the land grabber Gallagher and chased him around the field with the pitchfork.

"That's the meanest woman in Toornafrackin," he would say.

The truth was that Mary Kate was too wise for Grabber Gallagher's tricks. Had he not looked after the old "biddy" with cartloads of the finest turf in Ireland not to mention all the spuds and fresh milk? If it was a fair world no man had a better claim to the place than himself - or so he thought. Grabber had acquired four other small holdings in the neighbourhood and needed Quinn's place to join them all together.

Mary Kate was an odd individual all right. There was the time she put the litter of kittens in a sack and dumped them in a bog hole. By the time she got home the kittens were drying themselves in front of the fire.

I had been warned enough about the old woman's peculiar ways and trouble makings. It was a strange act of fate that made our paths cross that autumn morning.

The old bicycle groaned and squeaked as I pushed up the hill against a stiff breeze. Overhead the dark menacing clouds finally released their anger with an enormous downpour. It had been building up to it for about two hours. Lightening streaked across the sky, punctuated by the piercing rattle of thunder. I felt the rain going straight through to my skin. With my head bent against the elements, I barely heard Mary Kate call out from behind the green painted half-door.

"Come here young laddie or be God a Christ you'll be drowned," she shouted.

For a moment I could feel my heart pounding. It was no good trying to go on in the rain and storm. Dad had warned me about the danger of sheltering under trees during a thunderstorm. He had warned me too about Kate the Bush...

"I know you me bucko," she called out, at the same time waving her arm, "I want to see you a minute."

There was no escape for me - I felt trapped.

At first I could scarcely see through the thick acrid smoke, which filled every corner and crevice of the small living room. The ceiling and rafters hung with the thick black soot of generations. My nose twitched and I began to feel sick with the smell of something cooking. Once my eyes had adjusted to the blackness I was less frightened.

"Do you like chicken, laddie?" she enquired.

"Yes ... Yes I do," I replied rather nervously, trying to be polite and not upset the woman.

"Be God a Christ you can't beat a nice bit of chicken," she added.

My eyes fixed on the tin can boiling on the open fire.

I could see the feathers of the poor unfortunate half-plucked chicken as the lid bobbed up and down. Now I knew where the odd smell came from.

"It will soon pass over laddie," said Mary Kate, obviously trying to reassure me. I was beginning to think that maybe she wasn't a witch after all.

The old woman sat on a small wooden stool by the fire and sniffed a pinch of snuff from a tin box. This was Mary Kate's life. From this dark corner she would watch the world pass slowly by - the young ones growing old and the old ones die. The ticking of the old clock over the room door marked the passing days and years.

"Will you do me a big favour, Laddie?" she asked.

I nodded and wondered what was coming next.

"Bring me two pounds of bones from Fogarty the Butcher - it's all I can afford until pension day."

"I will," I replied feeling somewhat relieved.

"Do you like it then?" asked Mary Kate, interrupting my thoughts.

"Like what?"

"The clock"

"Oh yes . . . yes very much. It's beautiful."

"Be Jasus, it's like meself - been here for years and never shuts up."

I was quite enchanted by the old clock. The face of the clock was badly discoloured by the years of smoke and a safety pin and a tiny piece of valve rubber held the hands together.

This clock had a special place in Mary Kate's home. Here she kept what few valuables she possessed: her pension book; a few much fingered and faded letters and the dog licence. In the loneliness of her declining years she had come to regard it as almost a friend.

It had stopped raining now and the sky was beginning to clear. The clock struck eleven.

"I must be off now," I said, realising the time, "otherwise I'll be late for the Dispensary."

"Don't forget the bones," she shouted after me.

Old Fogarty sensed my predicament as I desperately searched for Mary Kate's pound. Both pockets were empty apart from a big hole, which had appeared in one of them. I started to panic - what would she say - no bones and, worse still, no money. I remembered her words:

"It's all I can afford until pension day."

"Lost your money, sonny?" he asked.

"It must have fallen through the hole in my trouser pocket." I replied, apologetically, half expecting the worst.

"Well never mind then, here you are," he said, handing me the brown parcel of bones.

Mary Kate was pleased and offered me a bowel of freshly made Chicken soup. I politely declined and left her sipping her soup in between mouthfuls of a Duff's batch loaf.

I didn't get the hiding I had expected from Dad after all. In fact my unplanned Good Samaritan act went down very well. Whenever I passed the way I enquired if she wanted any messages from the town. Usually the answer was yes - some of Fogarty's best bones for soup.

Grabber Gallagher never did get his hands on the land. In the end Mary Kate left it to a distant cousin that no one had ever heard of - at least it stayed in the family. Dad would bring the odd load of turf, which she appreciated.

I was lost in my thoughts when Mr.McGurke returned to the room with a green file.

"Sorry about the delay," he apologised, "must get this place sorted out."

"It's about the Will of the late Mrs. Quinn," said Mr. McGurke.

"Yes, I understand so." said my father.

"She has left the old clock to you - she wanted it to have a good home after all those years." he said.

My eyes lit up

"And when you get it home you will find it contains the price of a new bicycle for the boy." he continued.

I could feel a lump deep in my throat and my eyes began to fill up. Old Mary Kate would not be needing any more bones from Fogarty.

Mr Biddybaddy's Revenge

There were three houses at the end of our village - the peepers, the paupers and the gawkers. We lived in the middle one with the Peeper Towey's on one side and Gawker Galvin's on the other. Although they were nicknames they had a certain ring of truth about them. I think it must have been in the blood.

"There is nothing to be ashamed of in being poor," my father would say, "Jesus was a poor man wasn't he?"

I never really understood the comparison. Still, despite the torn Wellingtons, not to mention the exposed knees in my trousers and elbows sticking out of my jumper, I mainly enjoyed my youth.

Summer was my favourite time of the year. The school was closed for the summer holidays. In those day's summer seemed to stretch for an eternity. The laughter and shouts of the children kicking a football or playing a game of hide and seek in the evening was a delight.

Normally, life in our village was quiet and uneventful. We made our own amusement and the distinction between harmless mischief and downright blackguardism wasn't always apparent. The highlights of the year included bonfire night and Halloween but there were other occasions too like thrashing time, killing a pig and a visit from the hen woman.

The old school was a ramshackle place in the shadow of the mountain with high gable windows right up to the roof. There were holes in the floor and you could sometimes hear the rats career back and forth underneath the floorboards. The young Peeper's favourite trick was to put a crust of bread on a fishing hook and then wait for one of the rats to eat it. Peeper would then give the string a tug and when the rat squealed the whole class would be in uproar.

Old Master GILLIGAN, despite his inclination towards sadism at times, would be missed. He was a good teacher, if strict. The old Master wasn't really interested in sport and, anyway, the school couldn't even afford a football.

"Look! Over there," called out young Peeper's father, excitedly, one evening.

"Where?" says I, wondering if he had seen some sort of apparition.

"Flaherty's old place!"

"What about it?" I asked.

"Smoke, there's smoke."

"Is it on fire?" I enquired.

"No, no - there's smoke coming from the chimney."

He was right sure enough. It was a small, whitewashed house with a thatched roof above among the trees in the bog. It had been up for sale for about two years after old Flaherty passed away. It was said that the poor man drowned in a vat of whiskey on a day trip to Dublin with the Pioneers. The wake house was the biggest ever seen in the area and there wasn't a sober head in the place. You could smell the whiskey for about a week. Now it looked as if somebody was living in his old place again.

The days passed and the nights passed and the talking point of the village was the new resident. No one had managed to catch even a glimpse of him or her whichever it might be. Peeper and myself wondered if Flaherty had come back to haunt the neighbours. Even the Gawk GALVIN could not throw any light on the matter.

There wasn't much that happened in Drumgowna that was missed by the Peepers or the Gawkers. If one of them happened to miss a stranger passing the road the other was sure not to.

The curiosity aroused by not knowing the identity of the new occupant was bad enough but the shock of finding out was much worse. When Gawker's best cow ended up on her back in a drain it provided just the opportunity. Old Peeper was knocking on the door of Flaherty's asking for help before you could say Dinny's Sausages. What happened next was to leave a marked impression on his mind.

"Well who would have expected a black man in full tribal dress to answer the door?"

News of the new resident quickly spread like Finnegan's hay on the night of the big wind. Everybody was asking about the black fellow in the strange clothes who had recently come to live in Drumgowna.

"Maybe he's one of those Boluba fellows from the Congo?" said Peeper.

"Yes, perhaps he is a witch doctor?" I added.

"Well at least he won't have to do his rain dance in these parts," joked Gawker.

I cannot remember whose idea it was to play a trick on the unsuspecting visitor. It was planned with the precision of a military operation. Peeper climbed onto the roof quietly while I kept watch down below. The small shadowy figure of Peeper on the roof looked just like some demon silhouetted against the moonlit sky. After much pushing and pulling, he manoeuvred a large flagstone into position over the top of the chimney.

We hid in the ditch and waited for the fun. Sure enough, it wasn't long before the new resident came out into the dark night spluttering and coughing. I thought he was going to die. Then I wondered how he had managed in the Congo without any chimney at all.

Well, if that was a piece of blackguardism, it was nothing to what followed the next night. Peeper and myself got the biggest and most ferocious looking lump of bog oak we could find and carefully placed it up against the front door of the house. It's a great wonder the door didn't collapse under the weight of the thing. I attached a piece of string to the doorknocker and then trailed it to a point beyond the hedge.

"Rap! Rap! Rap!" went the knocker as Peeper tugged at the string. He was a wizard with a piece of string. He could easily have got a job in Duff's shop wrapping up the groceries in brown paper and tying the parcels with string. Almost immediately, the door opened lighting up the darkness and this great bog oak monster fell on top of the poor unfortunate man. He ended up on his back on the kitchen floor. The two of us scarpered off like a pair of devils across the fields.

"Help!" shouted Peeper, as he landed head first in a stream hanging by his trouser legs from a barbed wire fence.

When the stranger came to our door the next day and told my father what had happened, I was convinced he was a witch doctor. Only someone with supernatural powers could possibly have known that it was Peeper and me was responsible for such acts of blackguardism. Those two escapades earned me the biggest leathering I've ever had before or since.

Now it wasn't that I had anything against him because of his colour. Well, Heaven knows I had sent enough pennies to the black babies in Africa. My Uncle Patsy in London reckoned they must have got an awful lot of pennies judging by the number of them driving around that city in big cars.

Peeper was no brilliant scholar. For example, there was the time old Master Gilligan was giving a geography lesson and said to Peeper:

"Tell me boy, where is Uganda?"

"He's at home with me grandma." came the reply.

If the stranger thought he had been hard done by, he should spare a thought for the poor postman and count himself fortunate indeed. Every day he had to run the gauntlet of some of the most ferocious dogs in Ireland. I don't believe they had a licence between them. I was convinced our own dog knew instinctively when the postman brought bad news. But then any letter for our house was likely to be bad news - at least for the poor postman. The telegram boy came a close second and, of course, the village had long become a no go area for the Gardaí as far as the canine fraternity was concerned. It was a brave member of the Force who would come knocking on our door demanding to see a dog licence.

Soon it was September and back to school again after the long school holidays.

"Good morning, children." said Miss Doody.

"Good morning Miss." came the chorus of replies.

"This morning, children, we have a new headmaster."

The whole class waited eagerly.

"I'm sure you will like him - he has come a long way to teach in our school," continued Miss Doody.

"I would like you to welcome Mr. Biddybaddy who is on a secondment to the school."

Well, you can imagine my shock and horror. Peeper turned a funny shade of green and I thought he was going to be sick. Mr. Biddybaddy stood a full six foot six tall in front of the class. He wore a navy woolen jacket and smart grey trousers. Instead of a tie like old Master Gilligan, he wore a large colourful bow tie.

"What had happened to his funny African clothes" I wondered, trying to hide my face. He certainly looked very different now. The sight of him emerging from the smoke filled house coughing and spluttering flashed through my mind. I could feel the blood draining from my brain when I thought of our antics with Mr. Biddybaddy. My throat had gone dry and I too felt I was going to be sick. Miss DOODY's description of purgatory made the place sound attractive compared with the pickle I was in.

It all came as a great shock to me indeed. God only knew how I was going to survive it all and the outrageous things I had done to the poor man who surely had not deserved such treatment. I was feeling remarkably contrite and you would think to look at me that I was half way to Heaven.

I waited for the inevitable. The

schoolroom started to darken as a thick dark cloud blocked out the sun.

"All those stories about African witch doctors must be true," I thought, at the same time catching Peeper's eye. He was shaking all over.

"Stand up, Scully," the new master called out.

"Yes Sir." I replied sheepishly.

"I believe you are captain of the school football team?"

"I am Sir."

"Catch this then!" said Mr. Biddybaddy, at the same time throwing a brand new football towards me.

"I thought we should start off on the right foot," he said.

"From now on sport will be an important part of the school programme and I want this school to field a winning team - understood?"

"We won't let you down, Sir," I replied.

"That's right Mister - we won't let you down," added Peeper, who by now had stopped trembling.

"Maybe things weren't going to be so bad after all." I thought.

The Homecoming

The morning sun shone as the old man rested to listen to the cuckoo's song. He strained his failing eyes trying to catch a glimpse of her but she eluded him. "Ah May is a lovely time of year." he thought as memories of better times long past began to creep back from the deep recesses of his mind. Johnny Spellman had good cause to think of the past.

Today was no ordinary day. After all, he had waited and prayed long enough for Sean's return from England. Now his only son was at last returning to Gortlanain for good.

Suddenly, he realised how much work still remained to be done. The old place was beginning to look quite neat again. The neighbours had been a great help.

"I'm not as young as I used to be," he would say, acknowledging that the years were catching up on him. Sometimes his mind would wander.

"People can be so kind especially on occasions such as this," he thought to himself.

He winced with the pain in his back as he struggled to pull the last few nettles from around the barn despite Mrs. Roddy's protestations. She had called to give him a hand and was a good neighbour but a bit on the nosey side.

"Nettles are a stubborn breed if ever there was one." he thought to himself.

Mind you, it helped to be a bit stubborn to survive in that part of Ireland.

Years of hard work in all kinds of weather had made Johnny Spellman old before his time. Yet, it wasn't so much the hard work as the loneliness, which he found most difficult to bear. Maureen, his dear wife, had died a young woman. Her's was another story. Unlike the nettle, with its strength and stubbornness, she was one of nature's delicate flowers. She was an only child who lost her father before she scarcely had time to know him.

The old man's eyes started to fill up as he recalled her tales of milking six cows before school and carrying manure on her frail back. Her father's dying words were:

"Try and give her a good education, Maggie. She's not strong enough for the old sod."

The reality of farming life and the need to survive prevented that. Her health failed and eventually she could take no more.

His back was beginning to ache now as he replaced a few missing stones on the garden wall. The old sod, as he called the place, had been in his wife's family for generations. He married into the place having returned from years working in England. Now the clock had turned full circle. Sean was returning to stay. It had not been easy trying to scratch a living - more an existence really - all those years. If it hadn't been for the bit of seasonal work cleaning the river or turf-cutting on the bog he couldn't have managed. The few pounds from London helped too.

Sean had been a good son - the best any father could have reared. There was nothing at home to keep a young man there especially when all his mates had already taken the same road before him. All the promises of jobs and the big German factory had come to nothing. There was no shortage of promises but it was jobs that were needed. England offered the opportunity to earn some money and then return home perhaps.

"No one goes to England to stay," he reflected "but few ever seem to return."

Anyhow, that was in the past. Today, Sean Spellman was returning to the old sod to stay.

His thoughts strayed to the letter Sean had sent describing his work in London. In the early years those letters had been frequent and regular. Then, well... they started to drop off. He would watch the postman coming down the hill but he would keep going without stopping. "Good morning Johnny. No letter for you today, I'm afraid" he would say passing the time of day.

"It must be a great city for tunnels." he thought.

Sean was in the tunneling business. He had heard stories of the underground railway and often tried to visualise all those people criss-crossing the big city hundreds of feet below ground. Once more he stretched his back and drew his breath.

Things were going to be different now - so different. After twenty years his only son was returning to Gortlanain. All the neighbours and relatives would welcome him. Apart, and yet together, they had all grown older over the years. They would often ask for him - and he about them.

"How is old Robin Grady keeping?" he would ask in his many letters.

The old man's letters were harder to read now. His hand shook and the words sometimes played tricks with him. But Sean always knew what he meant. There was a mutual understating between them, which ran much deeper than the misspelt words, which filled the pages. News was scarce - the price of cattle, people dying and the odd wedding.

The old man always looked forward to his son's visits, which were the highlight of his year. Each year without fail he would make at least one trip. They had often talked into the small hours about the old place and the plans they had for it. Things were going well in England. He had managed over the years to get some money together. They would often laugh at the thought of Sean getting on the train on that cold January morning so long ago now with all his worldly possessions squeezed into a small suitcase no bigger than a large briefcase.

He felt a lump forming in his throat. Usually he would meet Sean at the railway station having hired a taxi for the return journey. Occasionally, Sean would make a surprise visit. In a way it was as though he had never left Ireland. Holidays were an opportunity to pick up where he had left off. In those early days England was a mere interlude in the otherwise continuous process that was his life - a life, which clinged to Ireland like the London mud which clinged to his boots. But time was to change all that.

There were friends to see and places to visit. Once more he would head off over the bog and down to the river to do a spot of fishing. For sure, the fishing was not as good as it used to be. Modern farming methods had polluted the rivers in Ireland just as they had done in England.

Above all else he loved the place - every bog hole and ditch; every tree and hedgerow.

He felt part of it and it was part of him. Apart from the inevitable signs of neglect in recent years the place had hardly altered.

Of course, life for Sean Spellman had changed too with the passing years. For one thing he was now a married man with two young children. The old man took a deep breath and quietly sighed.

"She was a nice enough person," he reflected "but why did he have to marry a divorced woman?"

He felt hurt at the time but tried to hide his feelings about the marriage.

Nevertheless, Sean sensed his father's disapproval. It wasn't so much what was said as what had been left unsaid. Sean felt hurt too about his wife's apparent rejection and for the first time he found himself torn between his father and the woman he had chosen to be his wife and to be the mother of his children. The relationship soured and the letters and visits became less frequent and then ... well... there was always some reason why they wouldn't be coming home.

Only the old man knew just how hard those years apart had been for him - years of waiting and hoping and believing. Anyway that was all in the past.

"What does it matter now?" he thought. "Who are we to judge others so cruelly when we can hardly attempt to understand the turmoil going on within their minds," he murmured forgetting for a moment that he was not alone.

He was becoming angry - angry with himself at the thought of all those lost years and missed opportunities. This was no time for anger, however, what was past was past now.

Like the shadowy waters, which flowed in the river, life carried on and on. It did not stop to allow time to disentangle confused emotions or permit a clearer view of events - and there was no turning back.

Lost in his private thoughts he was oblivious to the activity around the house.

"Come in for a good cup of strong tea, Mr. Spellman," shouted Mrs. Roddy, trying to get his attention.

"That man's hearing is getting worse and his mind is going too." she remarked under her breath.

Inside the house the smell of fresh paint filled the air. The glasses in the sideboard gleamed and the dresser was sparkling with its array of shining cups and saucers. A vase of freshly picked flowers decorated the kitchen table with its red and white chequered tablecloth. The kettle sang on the open fire like it had always done. There was a sense of stillness and peace in the place broken only by Mrs. Roddy hurrying about the house seeking out the last specks of dust.

"How are you feeling now, Mr. Spellman?" asked Mrs. Roddy.

"Ah grand. I'm feeling grand." he replied.

He did not feel very much like conversation as his mind tried to picture life here in Gortlanain with Sean and his wife and children. There was such a lot of work to do around the place. There were farm buildings to repair, fences to mend and drains to make. A tractor would make all the difference. The house itself was in a poor state. Sean would probably want to build a new one and take advantage of the government grant. He could put his pushbike away during the winter months now that there would be a car standing outside for his convenience. He hadn't noticed the time passing as he pottered about the house making last minute preparations for the homecoming.

Once more he heard Mrs. Roddy's voice calling out: "Johnny, Johnny, 'tis time you were getting yourself ready - the car will be here soon."

"What time is it Mrs.Roddy?" he asked.

"Ten o'clock - the flight is due at midday."

Quickly, he washed and tidied himself. He would wear his new suit - well it was two years old but still looked new - and his new shirt. He always looked smart and that much younger when he was dressed up.

His face was thinner now, his fingers twisted and his hands wrinkled. Struggling to scrape a living from between the rocks and the rushes had taken its toll. His mind was wandering more now. Some days he was good while on other days he was not so good. He would spend hours deep in his own thoughts sometimes. This was his very private world. That was the way he wanted it - intruders were not welcome.

Life had brought more than its fair share of ups and downs - "More downs than ups, perhaps." he sometimes felt.

Just when things were going well and he was beginning to get on his feet something would go wrong. Sometimes it was illness in the family, other times the death of a beast and, of course, the loss of his dear wife, Maureen. It seemed as though there was always something around the corner. Three score years had taught him that happiness was a very transient condition to be enjoyed while it lasted and then locked away within the private confines of ones most treasured memories.

Still, Johnny Spellman had accepted whatever God sent him as his own personal cross. He had agreed that with the Almighty a long time ago. That was the price he had to pay for bringing 'Dick the Gun' back to the sacraments. He had attended the Mission morning and night with that sole intention - that 'Dick the Gun" would go to confessions and start going to Mass again. If his prayers were answered he would accept whatever God sent. His prayers had indeed been answered.

Anyhow, this was no time to be feeling sorrowful. Had he not waited and wished for Sean's homecoming all those years. Ten years was a long time to be apart with only the promise of a visit next year or the year after. Promises... always promises. Now he was off to Knock Airport to meet his son once again. They had made up their differences and all was going to be well. Everything had changed now. Yes things were different now.

The grey mist was beginning to lift over Knock Airport as they carried Sean Spellman's coffin from the 'plane. He was coming home for good now and all his old friends were there to meet him. It was a fine turn out. In whispered conversations they'd asked how he died.

"Tunnel collapse," someone said.

The old man felt the comforting hold of Mrs. Roddy's hand on his arm as he wiped another tear from his face.

His mind was starting to wander again. All he had left now were his memories - what had been and what might have been. His heart felt heavy and his legs were growing weak. He hardly heard the words spoken as people shook his hand and offered their sympathy. He just wanted to be alone with his thoughts.

They said Gortlanain had never seen a funeral like it. Everyone was there. The sun was shining now making the air warm. A gentle breeze shook the tall Pine trees as the two coffins were laid side by side in the cold earth and Father Moran gave the last Blessing. No man can go on believing or hoping forever. Sooner or later he must face the truth however painful this may be. But now they were together at last - for good. They had both come home.

Darcy's Law

Garda Brian Mulcahy brushed the hairs off his brand new uniform before he ventured out into the snow and wind. The wind seemed to come at you from all directions. Cloghermore was a bleak and dismal place that, somehow, had been left behind by all the re-organisations and station closures. At least the people could thank O'Reilly the local TD for that much.

He had only been there a matter of weeks but he sometimes wished he was back in Dublin. He enjoyed Dublin. There was always something happening there - plenty of excitement and it was a lot warmer too. Cloghermore was just a small country village at the back of beyond as far as he was concerned. It was certainly no place for a keen twenty-two year old member of the Force.

The door opened and in came Sergeant Darcy.

"Morning Sarge." said Mulcahy.

"Huh, I don't know what's good about it Mulcahy - oh me head!" replied the Sergeant, obviously in some pain.

Mulcahy guessed this was probably self-inflicted. Sergeant Darcy was a man of about fifty years of age, overweight and wore a shabby uniform. He was one of the old time members of the Force. He liked to run things his way and his way was always the right way. In Cloghermore it was Darcy's Law that mattered.

"I think it's about time I had a few words of advice in your ear, young man." said Sergeant Darcy. "You're not walking the streets of Dublin now me lad. Things are different here – oh yes, very different."

"Well ... yes, I did notice things were a bit quiet all right." replied Mulcahy, wondering what was going to come next.

"Quiet is it?" shouted Sergeant Darcy. He moved closer saying almost in a whisper:

"It's so bloody quiet in this place, especially on the long dark winter's nights, that you can almost hear the dead sleeping in their graves."

"Yes Sarge."

"And don't keep on saying 'Yes Sarge'".

"Yes Sarge ... I mean, no Sarge".

People in Cloghermore were friendly by nature and feared rather than respected the Guards, as they were usually called.

"Keep your distance and don't get too familiar Mulcahy - especially with the girls."

Mulcahy nodded in agreement. One thing he had learned was that when Sergeant Tom Darcy said something, he meant it.

"And if you get any trouble from the youngsters around here don't waste your time with that reporting for summons business - kick them up the hole - that will sort them out."

Mulcahy was somewhat taken back.

"But Sarge, that amounts to assault!" he said.

"Look lad, I make the rules around this place. They know where they stand so you'll get no real trouble. When you're my age and looking forward to your pension and lump sum you don't want any bloody trouble - do you?"

"No Sarge",

That evening it was snowing heavily. Sergeant Darcy was typing away with two fingers at a desk near the open turf fire when Mulcahy returned. His hands were numb with the cold. He stamped his feet and shook the snow from his uniform.

"Stick the kettle on lad and make a cup of tae. It must be nearly an hour since I had the last one."

"Right you are Sarge - three spoons of sugar and well stirred" said Mulcahy as he filled up the kettle.

Guard Mulcahy couldn't help glancing over the sergeant's shoulder to see what he was typing.

"Have you arrested someone Sarge?" he asked with excitement.

"Of course not, you bloody fool - my arresting days are over," replied Darcy with apparent annoyance.

Garda Mulcahy saw that he had been typing an arrest report showing one Patsy Mulooly as having been arrested for stealing a mountain sheep.

"You see Sarge," added Mulcahy, "it's just that I was looking through the books the other day and noticed that no one has been arrested in Cloghermore in the last two years."

"How long have you been here now, Mulcahy?"

"Three weeks Sarge."

"Three weeks is it now. Well I've been here twenty years in this God forsaken place, looking at the same hills and the same faces day in and day out. I must know every sheep and goat from one end of the place to the other."

Mulcahy was sorry he raised the point at all.

"Still, it's a grand place if you can

stand the boredom and avoid trouble," continued the Sergeant.

Mulcahy thought he would pursue his point a little further and delicately enquired if there was any crime in the area.

"Of course there's bloody crime - the place is full of crime - sheep stealing, sheep shagging, poaching and poteen making. The bloody name was invented here. The place is alive with villains. The most despicable rogues and vagabonds in Ireland live in this place."

Darcy was obviously very worked up thought Mulcahy who was by this time intrigued about the whole situation. It was never like this when he worked in the big city. If you committed an offence you were summonsed or arrested as the case may be.

"Why are things different here?" he asked himself.

"If all these misdemeanors are being committed why are people not being arrested?" he enquired.

"The pull, that's why," replied the sergeant.

Mulcahy pursued the matter further, wanting to know what exactly Sergeant Darcy meant by the 'pull'.

"Politics me lad, politics. If there is anything the Irish are good at it is politics."

Mulcahy was puzzled. He was beginning to realise that perhaps he was not as well up in the ways of the world as he had imagined.

"Perhaps there were things to be learned even here in Cloghermore?" he thought.

"If you arrest or report someone for an offence - straight down to their local politician they go. A quick 'phone call and that's it - nothing is done." explained Sergeant Darcy.

Mulcahy protested that surely all this was corrupt and, indeed, sinful.

"Were politicians not people of integrity and respectability?" he wondered. "Do we not trust them to make important decisions, which affect our very lives?"

He seemed incapable of comprehending the existence of such unethical behaviour and devious dealings. Sergeant Darcy continued:

"Politicians and tourists are the real criminals. Well, I mean you have to be bent to be a good politician - it's part of the game. Tourists - well anyone who can afford to come here must be on the fiddle"

"I still think it's terrible that people can be so corrupt," said Mulcahy.

"Of course it is bloody sinful and corrupt. The whole world's corrupt - rotten to the core, and here are you and I trying to fight it". Sergeant Darcy laughed.

Mulcahy felt it was as though somehow he understood and accepted the situation as inevitable. He was still bewildered. His faith in society as a whole, not to mention the institutions of justice and politics, was badly shaken.

Sergeant Darcy started to type once more.

"But what about this arrest report you're typing, Sarge?"

"Administration lad - it's all to do with administration."

"Administration? I don't understand what you mean Sarge,"

Sergeant Darcy stopped typing again and started to explain:

"Well, it's simple isn't it? A record must be kept of all persons arrested and prosecuted so that statistics can be published in the Commissioners Annual report. Statistics, bloody statistics, that's what the job is all about today – nothing to do with catching villains."

Mulcahy was by now more confused than ever. Sergeant Darcy certainly had a strange way of looking at things but perhaps some of what he said made sense - to him at least.

"But how can you put in an arrest report if you haven't arrested anyone, Sarge?" he enquired, hesitatingly.

The sergeant looked at Mulcahy despairingly and with obvious annoyance.

"Well, we've got to show we're doing something haven't we, Mulcahy, - otherwise you and I, me lad, would be out of a job...now where's that tae you were makin..."

Beginner's Luck

Sean Fahey was one of life's losers when it came to girlfriends. The simple truth of the matter was that he didn't know how to talk to the female sex.

"Perhaps, I should have spent less time worrying about the farm and socialised a bit more," he pondered to himself.

Saturday night's Young Farmers' Dance was a typical example. He had wanted to ask Geraldine Moran for a dance but just couldn't bring himself to do so. She was a visitor to the area. The old feelings of self-consciousness and inadequacy returned. It wasn't his fault that he had two left legs.

"Why is dancing so important," he wondered, "women can be very cruel on the dance floor." He had learned that much from bitter experience.

"Geraldine Moran did not look the type to leave you stranded in the middle of the floor." he thought. He began to blame himself for his lack of personal courage. For a few moments Sean Fahey had forgotten about the farm.

He watched the shimmering reflection of the street lights in the roadway as he sheltered beneath the canopy over Flynn's drapery store. He could hear the rain drops beating hard against the canvas which flapped continuously in the wind. It was a wet and cold February evening and he felt the rain drops trickle down the back of his neck.

Sean leant against his bicycle for support and thought to himself, "What a time to decide to go to confessions". He was a man of routine if nothing else. As a little boy his mother, God rest her, had taught him to go at least once a month.

"What sins have I committed anyway," he thought "...chance would be a fine thing."

He glanced at the window display which seemed incredibly bright. Spring fashions had arrived. He couldn't help admiring the fashionably dressed, if rather expressionless, models that decorated Flynn's windows, adorned with the latest clothes from London, Paris and New York. These models seemed to stare out into the darkness at him and this made him feel uncomfortable. The rain continued to fall.

Sean was awkward in the presence of girls including the type you find in shop windows.

"Mind you, some of these look real enough", he smiled to himself. The rain was easing up slightly and people were beginning to move about under their umbrellas. The words of a poem from his schooldays about rainy nights came to Sean's mind. He couldn't remember the words although the teacher's slap across the back of the head was still quite vivid in his mind.

"No point waiting here any longer", he thought, as he straightened his cap and pointed his old bicycle in the direction of the church. Suddenly, in the corner of his eye he detected movement in the shop window.

"It can't have been, surely" he thought to himself, taking a closer look at the display. It was then that Sean noticed her staring at him from between the smartly attired models. Her clear soft features and short dark hair contrasted sharply with the cold expressionless faces of the shop models. Sean felt embarrassed and desperately tried to avert her gaze.

"Whatever will Geraldine think of me?" he asked himself.

Their eyes met briefly. She smiled gently in acknowledgement and continued to adjust the model's clothes. He could feel himself going into a hot sweat. His heart began to beat very fast.

"Well at least all the models were decently dressed." Old Mr.Flynn liked to maintain a proper sense of decency.

"Well, I mean, who had ever seen as much as one naked tailor's dummy in Flynn's shop window. There were those odd occasions in summer when, perhaps, there wasn't a great deal left to the imagination. Still, things were well within the bounds of respectability." Once more Sean thought about confessions. He noticed that the rain had almost stopped now.

As Sean Fahey cycled up the tree-lined avenue to the church he could picture the girl in his mind. She couldn't have been more than about mid-twenties, slim, with short dark nicely styled hair. She wore a fashionable woollen jumper with a wide black shiny leather belt over a long navy skirt.

Once more he felt uneasy and embarrassed about this encounter. "I wonder whatever she thought of me?" Sean asked himself.

He wanted to dismiss this fleeting encounter from his mind but couldn't, no matter how hard he tried. Geraldine Moran's smile, a warm and ... well, friendly, smile - kept haunting him.

Sean Fahey began to feel very sorry for himself again. Things just never seemed to click for him when it came to girls. He was certainly no James Bond but neither was he what you would call a bad looking fellow. It was just that he was downright awkward in the presence of the opposite sex.

"The only members of the female sex I seem to be able to get on with are either lifeless dummies or at least females in shop windows." he murmured to himself.

By the time Sean came out of church it was raining heavier than ever. He was about to get on his bicycle at the church gate when a voice shouted out of the darkness.

"Can I give you a lift, Sean?"

"Oh, it's alright thanks, I've got the bike with me," he replied as he tried to make out who was speaking.

"Don't worry about the bicycle, put it in the boot - terrible night to be on a bicycle, bygum."

"Yes ...yes, it is Michael, a terrible night sure."

Michael Reilly was from the next village.

"How nice of him to offer me a lift," he thought.

"Get in the back then, Sean, can't beat the old car when the weather's like this, can you?"

"No ... no, that's true," stumbled Sean, as he became aware of the young lady passenger in the front seat.

"Oh! Have you met my niece, Sean? Geraldine's down from Dublin. She's got herself a job in town. Decided to give her a lift - you know what the bus service is like, yes bygum."

The passenger turned around to say hello. Sean's heart skipped a beat as he recognised Geraldine Moran. As they looked at each other, Sean struggled searching for the right words to say. Now his mind was suddenly blank. He felt helpless as all his old fears came rushing back like a swollen stream in winter.

"Have you two met before?" enquired Michael.

"Well ...err ...not exactly."

"Lovely to meet you, Sean." said Geraldine in her rather soft lilting voice.

Sean Fahey nodded, still trying to think of something appropriate to say.

"Look, why not come over to my place for a chat and a drink. Geraldine doesn't really know many people around these parts." said Michael.

"Well yes ... if I'm not intruding, that is?"

"Intruding! – don't be a silly man."

Michael started the engine and switched on the windscreen wipers. By now Sean was beginning to feel a little more relaxed,

"I understand you're a keen fisherman, Sean. I'd love to hear about your fishing escapades?"

"Oh, I'm still just a beginner I'm afraid." replied Sean, somewhat surprised by her apparent interest.

"Well you know what they say about beginners luck," laughed Geraldine, as they drove off into the night.

Sean hadn't rated himself very highly as a fisherman but somehow he had a feeling deep inside that things were about to change.

A Grave Matter

It was a bitter cold January day. The snowflakes whirled to and fro, up and down, as if somehow possessed by some uncontrollable madness.

"A man could easily be lost on a day like this," thought James Patrick Mulvaney, as he pedalled his bicycle against a stiff breeze and the driving snow on his way to town.

He could get the pleasant smell of burning timbers in his nostrils. Little more than twenty minutes later and refuge was in sight - Flaherty's Pub. It seemed to beckon him to enter and he was certainly in no mood to argue. At least it would be warm there. Mary Anne Flaherty always kept a big log fire during the winter months - her Guinness was not all that good mind you.

Flaherty's was neat and tidy and, above all, a friendly place. Lost in the race for bigger, more modern, more profitable singing pubs, it was one of the truly old country public houses. It hadn't really changed very much since Mrs. Flaherty's grandmother's days. She, herself, only very reluctantly, agreed to have the "light" - it was certainly much cleaner than paraffin. At least now you didn't get the taste of oil when you sipped your pint.

Mrs. Flaherty had a passion for cleanliness.

"Cleanliness is next to Godliness," she would often say.

Of course, her idea of clean did not always accord with what others thought. A large open fire blazed away, fuelled by freshly cut logs which frequently spat sparks onto the sawdust strewn stone floor. The floor of the bar was flagged like the old kitchens of the past and was about six inches below street level. The ceiling hung low and what daylight did enter was scarcely enough even on the brightest of summer days - not to mention a day like today. This time of the year the kettle was permanently on the boil for hot whiskeys.

It was a small but cosy pub and certainly big enough for the customers nowadays. Gone were the fair days and market days when there was always a few shillings to be made. Mary Anne, however, was not one to complain or talk of better times now past. She still had a regular clientele if that was what you would call them.... These days her customers were the local drunkards, nutcases, wasters and anybody else who happened to be passing by and had the misfortune to call in.

He shook the snow off his Wellington boots and coat and warmed his hands with the heat of the fire.

"Give us a hot one, Mrs. Flaherty, if you please," he said.

On a day like this you certainly needed something strong to stop the blood freezing in your veins.

"No sooner said than done, James Patrick," replied Mrs. Flaherty.

A generous measure of whiskey, a dash of boiling water, add some sugar and a few cloves and you had the finest hot whiskey in the west of Ireland.

"Rather wintry this morning, Mr. Mulvaney," said Hughie McCormack, who was affectionately known in the locality as simply 'Cormack'.

Cormack was a small little man who spoke

with a soft, rather precise and somewhat effeminate accent. He'd had a good education but made little use of it - an education wasted if ever that was so. He always wore a gaily-coloured shirt with a wide round collar, which was a least three sizes too large. The knot of his tie finished some two inches short of the top button, which was usually open.

"Winter, spring, summer or autumn - what does it matter? People die and people are born," said John Joe Moran, at the same time bursting into a string of almost unintelligible utterances.

Poor John Joe lived in a world of his own and most of the time he was completely out of touch with reality. Some believed he was happier that way. He would chatter away to himself jumping from one subject to another without making any sense whatsoever. He was what you would call in these parts a real 'header' if ever there was one.

"Snowman, ploughman....Garret Fitzgerald ....good old Charlie .... Maggie Thatcher.... silver tea pot.... piss pot," continued John Joe.

It was never easy to grasp his words never mind attempt to make sense of them.

"Shut up you old ass," shouted Biddy McCann, at the same time bursting into a fit of hysterical laughter.

Biddy had seen better times. She wore a red coat, with an imitation fur collar, which didn't quite reach her knees and had obviously been made for someone half her size. She had a black scarf tied around her head and wore a pair of men's' Wellington boots with the tops turned down.

"You're a real martyr for the cause

Mr.Mulvaney, being out on a day like today," said Biddy.

James Patrick nodded his head in agreement and continued sipping his hot one as he stood with his back to the fire. The sooner they devise some form of central heating for bicycles the better he thought. He could feel the colour slowly returning to his cheeks.

Suddenly, the door burst open and in came Tombstone Gillespie who immediately ordered a large glass of 'Paddy'. Tombstone - he earned this name as a result of his propensity for grave digging - was white as a ghost and shaking from head to toe. He took two quick swigs and said " Same again missus". There was no mistaking that his behaviour was extremely odd.

"What's up then, Tombstone?" said Cormack.

"I'd rather not say if you don't mind," he replied. He always had a sharp answer.

All this was too much for the assembled company.

"Look here, Tombstone, you've known us all these years so you can tell us," said Biddy.

"Your secret is safe with us," said Cormack, who was the last person anybody would tell if they had a secret to reveal.

Now if there was one thing that the regular customers of Mary Anne Flaherty's pub could not resist it was a bit of local gossip or scandal. The truth or otherwise didn't really matter so long as the story was good. Their motto was "Don't let the truth spoil a good tale". Tombstone was known as one for a good leg-pull but on this occasion he seemed dead serious.

The others moved closer in anticipation of what Tombstone had to tell. He glanced around the bar as if to see who might be listening and then commenced to tell his story.

"I've been digging graves for the past twenty years but have never seen what I saw this very morning. God knows the heart is crossways in me mouth."

A deathly hush seemed to fall on the place broken only by the sound of the timbers burning on the fire. Tombstone paused as if in deep thought and wiped his brow.

"Go on then, don't keep us in suspense," said Biddy.

"There it was staring me in the face. The skull and bones of some poor soul with a silk tie knotted around its neck." said Tombstone.

"Silk tie is it Be God. Sure who's ever heard of a corpse being buried with a silk tie around its neck?" said John Joe, once again bursting into a litany of non-senseical words and phrases.

"Shut up, John Joe and let him finish his story." said Cormack.

Tombstone described how he had been digging Pat O'Reilly's grave when he came on the bones and noticed that a silk tie had been knotted around the neck. He took it off and cleaned it up and it was clearly silk tie - even the colours of the stripes, which were red and green, were distinctly visible.

"Now why would old Mrs.O'Reilly have been buried with a tie around her neck?" Cormack asked.

"Sure where would they get a silk tie is more to the point." added John Joe, once more breaking into one of his frequent outbursts.

"Tie me kangaroo down boy.... God Bless John Mitchell ... transportation.... C.I.E...."

"But that's where your all wrong - it wasn't the remains of poor old Mrs. O'Reilly," said Tombstone. "Her remains were further down."

"Glory be to God and His Holy Mother," said Biddy "and who was it then?"

"Well who indeed?" said Cormack, "There should only be one body in that grave."

It was then that the full significance of the gruesome affair really dawned on them. An unknown corpse buried in Mrs.O'Reilly's grave with a silk tie around its neck. Poor Mrs.O'Reilly, God rest her soul, had died some twenty years earlier and who dug her grave but Tombstone. Therefore, the second body must have been added later. The knotted tie around the neck could mean only one thing - strangulation - that meant murder.

"I'll go for the guards this very minute." said Commack, jumping from his stool and making for the door like a hare before a hound. He had never been seen to move like that before.

"Come back here you fool." shouted John Joe.

"That's right." said James Patrick "We don't want this news to get out. Just imagine - guards climbing all over Mrs. O'Reilly's grave not to mention detectives down from Dublin and all those pressmen."

Mrs. Flaherty was, of course, quick to mention the trade it would bring and God knows how much that was needed.

"No," said Tombstone, quite emphatically, "The bones and tie have been put in a bag and re-buried. As far as I'm concerned I don't want any of you - including you, Cormack - to as much as breath a word of this to anyone."

Tombstone was clearly shocked by his experience and, on reflection, no one really welcomed the thought of a big enquiry. Above all, the family of the poor soul who was to be buried in the same grave after 10 o'clock Mass in the morning would hardly appreciate it. So it was decided that nothing would be said - the dead would be allowed to rest in peace.

By now it was time to think about going home and it was still snowing hard outside. Nobody had noticed the stranger who had entered until he cleared his throat and called for a large pint for a terrible thirst! Strangers were regarded with some suspicion around these parts and a great deal of curiosity.

Cormack could not resist asking him for a light while at the same time eyeing him up and down. He was tall, medium build, had dark hair, glasses and . . . wore a red and green striped silk tie…

Cornelius Clancy
and the Land of the Fair Ones

We laid old Clancy to rest the other day. Father Moran gave him a grand send off. The sermon was all about life - he hardly mentioned death at all! Sure Clancy himself would have loved it.

Now that he has gone to his eternal reward I can tell you of a strange story he told me many years ago. He made me swear that I would not tell a living soul until he was six feet under and pushing up the daisies in the graveyard above in Lisnashee. I've kept that promise all those years.

When Cornelius Clancy was a young fellow he was a bit wild. He was always up to some form of devilment. It's a great wonder he was never locked up in Mountjoy Prison or in some similar establishment for his antics.

There was the time Dooley ploughed a big field in the morning being very careful, of course, not to touch the old ring-fort. When he returned after his dinner the whole field was back to grass again! Dooley blamed the fairies at first but everyone knew it was none other than me brave Clancy.

Now it is that ring-fort at Lisnashee, which brings me to the point of my story - or should I say, Cornelius Clancy's story. This is the way he told the story to me. The old people of the village would always say that if you went into the cave in that fort in Dooley's field you would travel for miles underground and come out somewhere in the middle of Lough Gara. On the other hand you might never be seen again. The story seemed to have the desired effect in that no one ever attempted to discover the truth or otherwise - except me brave Clancy.

One fine summer's day he decided to explore the cave taking with him a pair of Wellington boots and an old storm lantern. The cave was dark and wet with droplets of water dripping from its corbelled stone roof. After a short while he came to what appeared to be the end of the cave. Now Clancy was not one to give up easily. He pulled and pushed at the stones blocking his way until, eventually, he was able to dislodge enough stones to remove a large upright flagstone that formed a kind of door. It's a great wonder the whole structure did not collapse on top of him.

He removed the flagstone door, which lead to a long passageway, which he followed, bumping his head as he went. Before very long he found himself in the middle of a beautiful valley. There were lush green pasture fields full of wild flowers of every kind you could possibly imagine and each with a scent that would do your heart good. There was an abundance of fruit of all types on the trees. Birds of every size and colour were there and their singing would do you the power of good. The trees were as tall as the Kerry Mountains and covered with blossoms of all different colours.

A river ran through the valley and it was clear and full of fish of all different kinds. There was brilliant sunshine and even when it rained nothing ever got wet. Clancy was enchanted by this wondrous place, which was not like any place he had ever seen before.

After enjoying these marvelous sights for a while, he decided he would look to see if there was anybody about. Soon he laid eyes on the most pleasing sight you could ever hope to see. There were hundreds of beautiful women, each one with long golden hair down her back, cheeks the colour of a foxglove and eyes like the bluebells in the wood. At first, Clancy admired these scantily dressed young women from a distance, not wishing to interrupt their work. As he got nearer, he realised that they all looked very sad. They did not smile or laugh or show any expression of joy.

They told him of their sad plight. A witch had entered their land one night when they were fast asleep and stolen their pot of gold. Until the gold was returned they could never smile again and great sadness would be upon their hearts.

"Well that is a cruel fate, sure enough." said Clancy.

"We will take you to our Queen. She knows where the gold is hidden." they said.

He readily agreed to meet the Queen for if she was anything like themselves she would be a sight to behold.

"Welcome Clancy of the red hair and strong arms." greeted the Queen.

"Thank you mam." says Clancy, feeling rather unsure of himself.

"It is a great misfortune has fallen upon our people losing our gold as we did." said the Queen.

She explained to Clancy how the gold had been in the possession of her people in the Land of the Fair Ones for thousands of years and how life in the land had been so peaceful and joyful. Then, about a thousand years ago or so, a witch had entered their land and stolen it. Since that day great sadness had fallen upon her and her people who were full of grief and anguish.

"I see now." said Clancy, feeling rather puzzled about the whole affair.

"Will you help us, please?" pleaded the Queen.

"And how can a poor fellow like me self help you?" asked Clancy.

"You can go to the place where the gold is hidden and bring it back to us."

"And sure can't you go and get it yourselves?" enquired Clancy.

"No, if we touch the gold while it is in your world it will turn into stone immediately."

All this was becoming a bit too much for me brave Cornelius Clancy who was now regretting that he had ever ventured into that cave in Dooley's ring-fort.

"We will reward you well if you agree to help us." added the Queen.

"You can have the choice of: a share of the gold; the wife of your own choosing or the gift of knowledge." added the Queen.

"You are very generous I must say." replied Clancy.

"But you must return all the gold exactly as you find it." she said.

He considered the matter for a while but the thought of all those beautiful women spending eternity without a smile on their faces or joy in their hearts was too much so he agreed to help and a plan was devised.

"There is one more condition," said the Queen, "You must never think an evil thought or speak an unkind word or do any bad deed towards my people."

After what seemed like many days, Cornelius Clancy returned from the Land of the Fair Ones and set out to find the hidden gold. To his surprise he had only been away for little more than an hour! It was not long before he found the gold exactly as described.

Then he thought of all he could buy with so much gold.

"I could build a new house and buy cattle and land and, perhaps, a tractor." he thought.

He would never have to want for anything again. But then he remembered the beautiful young women in the Land of the Fair Ones and their Queen and recalled their sad faces. Quickly he dismissed these thoughts from his mind.

Clancy returned to the Land of the Fair Ones again and there was much rejoicing and celebration at the return of the gold. The Queen and her people were happy once again and it was all thanks to the bravery of Cornelius Clancy and to his honesty in keeping his promise to return all the gold. The festivities lasted for a hundred days and nights and then the time came for him to choose his reward.

"And what now Clancy do you wish as your just reward?" asked the Queen.

"That is a difficult choice for me to make." he said.

"You must choose now unless it is your wish to remain in the Land of the Fair Ones forever."

"Very well then," says he "I will choose a wife from your people for surely I have never laid eyes on any woman as beautiful as the women of this land." replied Clancy.

After picking his bride he bid farewell to the Queen and her people and the Land of the

Fair Ones and they set out for Lisnashee. After some time they came to the mouth of the cave in the ring-fort. It was then that a strange thing happened.

For as soon as the feet of his new bride touched the earth outside the fort she immediately turned into a large stone. Then Cornelius Clancy remembered how he had thought about what he could buy with so much gold.

Well to cut a long story short, as they say, that was the end of Clancy's bride from the Land of the Fair Ones. If you should happen to visit his place in Lisnashee you will see a large stone in the front garden covered with beautiful flowers planted and tended by his own hand ... or so he would have you believe!

Once Before I Die

Doctor Cronin stopped tapping at his new computer, swung around on his chair and stared at John Joe McGinley. He hesitated before he spoke.

"I'm afraid, I have some bad news for you, Mr.McGinley."

John Joe felt his heart beating faster.

"Is it me heart, Doctor?" he enquired anxiously.

"No, it's not your heart but you are very ill."

"How serious is it?" he begged.

"I'm afraid it is too late for me to do anything for you."

The words hit him like a bolt of lightning and he could feel the walls closing in around him. He had not stood in a doctor's surgery since he was a youngster, and now! Although still only forty-five he looked more like sixty years old.

Yes, he could have looked after himself better. He knew that all right. Perhaps, his reputation in the village as a skinflint was justified. He couldn't see the point in wasting hard earned money on doing up the old place and buying smart clothes. If it wasn't for Breedge Donnelly bringing him his Sunday dinner he probably would have starved long ago.

"How long have I got?" he enquired.

"Three months - maybe less, it depends."

The doctor had been straight with him at least. It had come as a great shock but now he knew. If the pain in his chest had not got worse he would not have gone to see the doctor at all.

"Three months to live ... just three bloody months."

He was angry, angry with the world and angry with himself.

"Can this really be happening to me," he wondered "or is it just another nightmare?"

John Joe McGinley had enough nightmares in his time - especially after a night putting the world right on the corner stool in Fagin's pub. That was years ago now and had he not mended his ways since those reckless rakish days.

McGinley was not very popular with the villagers. He was the type that would fight with his own toenails - a real brier if ever there was one. If it wasn't the swans from the river eating his grass, it was the children's laughter and shouts of youthful exuberance affecting the cow's milk yield. His habit of criticising the neighbours and especially the clergy annoyed them. He had not seen the inside of a church for years.

Now the springs of life were weakening. Had John Joe McGinley been cast in kindlier times he might have risen to assume a brighter role in life's affairs.

John Joe was a confirmed bachelor - or was he? He knew Breedge Donnelly had an eye for him over the years. She was a kindly soul and he enjoyed her sense of humour. Anyway, being stuck above in the middle of the bog with the crows was no place for a woman like her. The years of neglect were evident with grass growing on the old thatch roof and the smoke coming out the front door.

He tightened the piece of baling twine tying his heavy black overcoat and straightened his thick woollen hat from under which tufts of curly hair protruded.

The wind was blowing quite strongly now as he made his way along the wood road from town.

Again, he began to think about his life or what was left of it. It had been a lonely life and, perhaps, he must take much of the blame. If John Joe McGinley had been a grumpy neighbour it was because most of the time ... well. . he felt grumpy.

"Three months - maybe less."

Doctor Cronin's words again echoed in his ears. Now he could feel the pain once more. He would go back to see the doctor next week.

"John Joseph McGinley, late of Letterfrack, died in the County Hospital. Funeral to take place after 12 o'clock Mass..."

John Joe could just see the death notice. Suddenly, it dawned on him. There would be none of those modern funeral parlour places for him. They were too cold and impersonal. He wanted to be among his friends - but what friends?

Then there would be the corpse house. The old place was a disgrace. You could scarcely see yourself in the smoke. The ceiling was black with soot and what remained of the curtains had changed to a peculiar shade of creamy brown.

He stared at his unshaven face in the cracked mirror and hardly recognised himself. He would need to tidy himself up and get some new clothes. Even in death a man had his dignity. Soon he would be shaking hands with St.Peter. It might even be Old Nick himself with the life he had led. John Joe McGinley decided that he would have to turn over a new leaf.

When McGinley entered Fagin's public house

nobody recognised him at first. The neat haircut together with a smart brown sports jacket and matching trousers made him look a completely different person.

"I don't believe it - it isn't - it is! John Joe McGinley." exclaimed Breedge Donnelly as she took a quick sip of her hot whiskey. Mind you, she'd always thought he was a fine looking man if only he had looked after himself and kept up his appearance.

"Hello Breedge." he said, rather shyly and feeling a little awkward.

"This is a surprise. We don't often see you in this place these days." replied Breedge.

"No. no -I've been keeping me self to me self you could say."

"Well it is certainly good to see you anyway and you're looking so well".

"Little does she know?" he thought to himself.

It was ironic really. He knew Breedge Donnelly had a bit of an eye for him but he was never really interested. They had passed the time of day and he enjoyed the hot dinners but that was it.

John Joe had enjoyed the evening drowning his sorrows in a few pints of Fagin's best Guinness. Breedge was good company especially when she had a few drinks. For a while he had forgotten his own troubles.

The very next day he set about making plans for his impending demise. The house would be given a complete overhaul including a new roof. Yes, he would replace the old thatch. Moran, the sweep, would clean the chimney. A new coat of whitewash would finish the job off together with a good tidy up outside.

For days the talking point of the village and villages around was the change that had come over John Joe McGinley. He dressed smartly and shaved every day. Already the workmen had stripped the thatch and were putting on a new slate roof. Fogarty, the local shopkeeper, could hardly believe his ears when McGinley said he wanted to pay off at once all the money he owed for groceries. Rumour even had it that John Joe McGinley had even paid for a round of drinks in Fagin's. After Mass on Sunday he was seen talking to all the neighbours and put a pound in the collection. Instead of shouting at the school children he gave them sweets.

The transformation was nothing short of remarkable. However, only he knew the reason for the sudden change.

"Perhaps now they'll realise I was not so mean and miserable after all." he thought.

"I was ... well ...I was wondering Breedge if you would be interested in going to the annual farmers' dance tomorrow night?"

Somehow, he had managed to pluck up enough courage to ask the question.

"Oh ... I hadn't really thought about it." she replied somewhat surprised.

"It's just that I haven't been to a dance in years." she continued.

"Well, I thought maybe we could just go along, have a drink and a chat and listen to the music."

"Yes ... Yes, of course - I'd love to."

"Great. I'll pick you up at about eight."

In all the years she had known John Joe McGinley and kept a soft spot for him she had never known him to ask her out. Still, she was certainly not complaining. If he had turned over a new leaf then, as far as she was concerned at least, that was all for the better.

He had always admired her. She was more the sensible type - not like some of those smart young things about these times. You wouldn't get one of those milking a cow or scattering - a bit of manure.

"I'm glad I asked her out at least once," he thought to himself, "Yes, just once - once before I die."

"Come in." said a voice as John Joe knocked on the surgery door.

"Ah...Mr ...err...?"

"McGinley".

"Ah yes - Mr. McGinley. Sit down."

He sat nervously on the chair as Dr.Cronin tapped away at his computer.

"Right, Aloysius Joseph McGinley." he muttered to himself.

"Excuse me, doctor," interrupted John Joe, somewhat nervously.

"Yes, what is it then?"

"It's my name ..."

"Yes, of course, it's your name."

"No, I mean the Aloysius Joseph bit."

"Your name is McGinley, well isn't it?" the doctor retorted.

"Yes, but there's no Aloysius."

"No Aloysius! No Aloysius! What do you mean man?"

"I mean my name's not Aloysius Joseph, it is John Joseph McGinley."

Dr.Cronin was angrier than ever now. How dare a patient query what was on his brand new computer.

"Well who is Aloysius Joseph McGinley then?" enquired the doctor.

"He lived over the hill in Pullbawn - we

70

buried him last week," replied John Joe.

A long silence followed as Dr.Cronin continued to play with his computer.

"There's been a terrible mistake, Mr McGinley."

"Mistake!"

"I'm afraid the records have been ... well, mixed up."

"You mean...?"

"Yes."

"And I'm not going to die in three months?"

"That's right - unless you get run over by a tractor load of turf on the way from the bog!"

John Joe McGinley felt as light as a feather as he made his why home. The pain in his chest had gone. Dr. Cronin's indigestion tablets had done the trick. Now he couldn't wait to tell everyone his story, especially Breedge Donnelly.

"Oh John Joe McGinley, you are a one all right, you and your indigestion." said Breedge, as she sipped another hot whiskey before the big turf fire in Fagin's.

"I was wondering..." he said, breaking off in mid-sentence…

"Yes, John Joe?"

"...I was just wondering if you would be interested in hanging out your washing on my clothes line..."

They both smiled.

Out of the Frying Pan

Michael Roache did not like driving at night - especially on dark stormy winter nights. It was late and he felt compelled to drive on. There was still another forty miles to go and the roads were bad.

He wished that the meeting had ended earlier. His mind turned to Anne and his two beautiful children. He recalled them saying "Don't be late Daddy". The car was suddenly caught in a strong gust of wind blowing across the lake and almost ended up in the ditch.

"It certainly is a wild night." he thought to himself and switched on the car radio.

It was nine o'clock and he had just tuned in to the news in time to hear:

"Gale force winds gusting to hurricane strength are now sweeping the west of Ireland. Intending travellers are advised not to make their journeys unless absolutely necessary..."

Michael instinctively increased speed.

"If only I had another hour I could be home." he wished. By now he was conscious of what Anne would be thinking. She too would probably have been listening to the news.

"Just my luck to get caught up in a storm." he thought to himself.

For some reason he glanced at the fuel gauge and noticed that it was almost on the empty mark. He wished he had thought to fill up before leaving.

"The storm is getting really bad." he thought.

Suddenly, as he rounded a sharp bend he saw in the light of his headlamps a large tree, which had crashed onto the road. Quickly, he braked managing to stop just in time.   Michael wiped the sweat from his forehead and breathed a sigh of relief.

"Phew!   that was a bit too close for comfort," he gasped.

It was now becoming obvious that there was little point in trying to get any further. What he needed was somewhere to shelter until the storm died down. In any case, all the roads in the area were likely to be blocked by falling trees.

Through the swaying fir trees Michael noticed the flickering lights of what appeared to be a large house. A narrow roadway, with trees on one side and a fast running stream on the other, lead up to what he could now see was a hotel. It was a large old-fashioned two-storey building, which gave the appearance of being rather run down.

"Perhaps my luck's not too bad after all," he mused.

Michael Roache's eyes fixed on the large wooden door, which looked as if it had not been opened for years. There was an uncanny feeling about the place.

"I can't imagine many tourists visiting this place." he thought.

Although, he felt some reassurance on seeing the lights through the windows he still felt uneasy. The hotel was dark and somewhat pokey inside. There seemed to be lots of nooks and crannies and he could almost taste the cigarette smoke in the air.

"Come and join us won't you, dearie," called a rather deep female voice from somewhere near the counter. The lady in question came up to Michael and indicated that he should take off his coat.

"You will be staying a while with us won't you?" she enquired.

The ripple of laughter from the rest of the assembled crowd did not escape his notice.

"It's a bad night outside. The road is blocked further down." replied Michael, conscious of the fact that he was speaking very fast and feeling a little unsure of himself.

She was a rather heavily built lady to put it mildly. The notion of husband beating seemed more plausible, somehow. "Fancy being married to her," he thought to himself.

Thoughts of home and family again passed through his mind. The whole building seemed to shake with every powerful gust of wind and to Michael, home seemed a long way off.

He looked around to try and find another member of the male sex, feeling decidedly uncomfortable in the presence of this gathering of women.

"A pint of Guinness, if I may please," he called rather timidly.

Michael was now becoming increasingly more self-conscious as he desperately looked around for a friendly face. No sooner had he sat down by the large open fire and taken a sip of his Guinness when a voice interrupted his moment of quiet reflection. The lady with the rather gruff voice called out:

"Are we ready to start then, ladies - we mustn't keep Mr.Roache waiting must we?"

He could feel a cold shiver run down his spine at the sound of his own name being called. Michael's feelings of discomfort quickly changed to a sense of sheer horror.

"What is happening to me?" he asked

himself.

Before he could even attempt to answer his own question, Michael Roache found himself being propelled into the middle of the room by three women ably assisted by the lady with the gruff voice. All the other women seemed to be gathering around in a menacing manner. He realised that the mood of the group had now changed dramatically and he was suddenly the principal actor in some strange ritual that he could not understand. He had not experienced real fear until this moment.

"What's happening? What have I done?" he demanded as he attempted in vain to break free from their grip.

There must have been at least thirty women of different ages present and not as much as one man - other than himself, of course. He wondered if it was some sort of practical joke or, perhaps, a case of mistaken identity.

"How do they know me?" he wondered.

Some of the women were screaming, others sobbed uncontrollably, while more just laughed and pointed their fingers at him in a jeering manner. He felt a great anger directed at him, which he could not comprehend. Nothing seemed to make sense anymore. He could feel his stomach turning over and over and over...

Michael searched desperately for a possible escape route but could not find one. He felt trapped and absolutely helpless.

"Why me - what have I done?" he kept asking himself.

He wished it was all just some horrible dream but it was all too real. He felt himself losing consciousness ...going ...going...

He woke up to the sound of running water. His clothes were torn and he felt sore all over. He rested for a short while by the stream which passed under the road bridge and ran into the lake. The storm had ceased and he thought how nice the water looked in the early morning light. Michael's mind was confused as he tried to gather his thoughts. Then he noticed the fallen tree, which still blocked the road and immediately thought about the storm.

All sorts of memories were triggered in his head as he tried to disentangle and make sense of events. Now, his main concern was to seek help and to get home - home to Anne and the children. He did not stop to see what had happened at this strange old worldly hotel. Without looking back he hurried along the road hoping to find someone - anyone who could help.

It wasn't very long before Michael met a local farmer. Michael told his strange story about the hotel and the odd goings on. The farmer listened with a rather puzzled and somewhat surprised expression on his face.

"Ah there's no hotel down there me lad - not for years there hasn't been one." said the farmer.

"Well maybe it was just a pub," retorted Michael.

"No pub, neither. No pub and no hotel."

Michael was becoming angry now and was certainly in no mood for a joke.

"But there is I tell you. Where do you think I spent last night while the storm was raging?"

Michael felt confused now and began to

wonder if his mind had been playing tricks on him.

The farmer sensed his apparent desperation.

"You see, me lad, there's an old story told in these parts that once a year the souls of the dead women gather in the valley below and lament their years of suffering at the hands of drunken and cruel husbands. They..."

"Look! Look! below in the valley ... fire ..."

"Ah they'll be a peace now, God rest them."

"You mean..."

"Yes, no hotel and no fire."

Michael tightened the scarf around his neck as he felt a cold shiver run through his whole body. The farmer slowly puffed his pipe and then looked Michael straight in the eye with a slight hint of a smile on his face, saying:

"You weren't to know, me lad, but when you followed those lights last night - you were going from the frying pan into the fire."

Michael shook his head in bewilderment. He was beginning to see things a little clearer now - well at least he thought he was...

"Anne will never believe this," he thought.

Love is a Perfect Stranger

"You'll have to get yourself a nice girl." His mother's words rang in his ears as he continued to turn over the wet turf.

"It's easy for her to talk," he thought "After all what can I hope to offer any girl - a few acres of wet bog land and a few head of cattle."

Girls were a sore subject with Michael Corcoran. He just didn't seem to be able to talk to them. In simple terms he was, to put the point bluntly, a failure. He got on all right with the country girls but then there weren't too many of those left now. They had got good jobs in Sligo and Galway and those who remained were usually spoken for or so it seemed.

Michael would go to the usual local dances in the town but then that was his second problem - he couldn't dance very well.

"Anyway, those town girls are a little bit too smart for my liking," he mused. "They just look down on us country fellows." he thought aloud. There was that element of snobbishness about them he felt.

His back was beginning to pain now from all the bending. He straightened up and drew his breath taking in the heather-perfumed air. Michael listened for the sound of the one o'clock train as it puffed its way into town and which for him was the usual signal for dinner.

"I could certainly eat something now." he thought.

The white fleecy clouds drifted across the blue sky and he could feel the soft breeze on his cheeks.

Cloonmore bog land lay between the river and the railway line with only a cart track linking it to the village. Beyond the railway lay Feeney's Wood and beyond that again the main road into town.

"There's good drying today," he thought to himself "if this keeps up it should be ready for footing by the weekend."

He was so deep in his own thoughts that he scarcely noticed the figure of a young girl coming over the hill from the direction of the river. He was not used to seeing members of the fair sex here in the middle of Cloonmore bog. His company was more likely to be the bilberries and bog cotton, which abounded.

"Perhaps it is some form of mirage," he wondered, but no it was real enough all right. He could see her clearly with her long dark hair blowing in the breeze.

Michael pretended not to notice as he continued his work. He couldn't help wondering what a girl was doing here in the middle of nowhere. Occasionally he would give a quick glance up, as she got nearer.

"Excuse me, I seem to have got a little lost," she called out, rather apologetically.

"Oh hello there," replied Michael, as if this was perfectly normal encounter.

"I've been walking along the river and should have turned off towards Feeney's Wood for the road back into town but I think I have gone too far," she continued.

Michael stopped working and stood up again.

"Ah you're miles out of your way I'm afraid." he said.

He felt his back ache as he stood with his hands on the small of his back to ease the pain.   He noticed her red cheeks and beautiful fresh complexion. She was dressed in casual clothes and somehow looked at home among the wildness of the place.

"Oh let me introduce myself - I'm Sally."

"Pleased to meet you, I'm Michael Corcoran. I live across the way."

"You see, I thought I would follow the river, as it was such a lovely day, and then cross the fields to the wood and back along the road."

"You must have been walking for a long time?"

"Yes - I didn't realise there would be so many ditches and drains to cross." she said laughing.

"It's like that in the country, you know," said Michael.

"So I gather."

Sally watched as Michael continued to turn over the wet sods which stuck to the burnt heather. His fingers too were beginning to feel sore.

By now he was starting to feel uncomfortable with the conversation. Michael wondered what she thought about him and if she sensed his embarrassment. Hopefully she didn't think he was being unfriendly. It was just that he wasn't much good at chatting up girl - especially those upstarts from the town! Somehow he always seemed to dry up and would feel himself blushing.

"Do you mind if I have a go at that?" she asked, taking him somewhat by surprise.

Michael stopped working again.

"Of course you can but it's severe on the hands - and the back."

He quickly showed her what was required and soon they were both at it hammer and tongs so to speak.

Michael Corcoran was amazed that a girl from the town would want to try her hand at something like that. He was surprised too that she managed to do it so well.

"Maybe those town girls are not so different after all," he thought to himself.

Her slim figure and flowing hair made a pleasant sight against the background of the turf and heather.

Suddenly, she stopped turning the turf and he could see that she was rubbing her eyes.

"Oh dear, I'm sorry. I appear to have something in my eye," she said, obviously in some discomfort.

"It is probably dust from the turf. Would you like me to have a look?"

"Please do," she replied, at the same time taking out her handkerchief.

Michael could feel his heart beating faster now. Taking a speck of dust out of someone's eye was a simple enough process but this was different. She was a girl and Michael was not used to dealing with girls. All the same, this was something of an emergency.

Michael looked into her eye using his thumb and forefinger to gently prize the eyelids apart. Her right eye blinked a great deal and he could see that it was very watery, right enough, there was a tiny piece of dust in the corner.

"Try closing your eye and moving your eyelid back and forth." said Michael. She willingly obliged.

When she opened her eye again he could see that it was still very watery and squinting a lot but there was no sign of the dust.

"Give it a wipe with your hanky as it's

cleaner than mine." he said. She wiped her eye and began to feel much better.

"Thanks - I guess I'm not used to this work.".

For a moment both stood looking into each other's eyes. Michael couldn't remember ever standing that close to any girl before. He hadn't really thought about it while he was helping to get the dust out but now he was feeling very self-conscious again. He felt embarrassed and could easily have run away. Sally smiled and he could feel himself smiling also. It made him feel a little more relaxed.

It was only at that moment that he really had a chance to fully appreciate her natural beauty. Her large bright blue eyes seemed to sparkle in the sunlight and her face was fresh and radiant. It was a pleasure to see such beauty without any use of make-up. Her dark thick brown hair was curly as if shaped by the fairies that played among the bog cotton when the moon was high.

Suddenly, she leaned forward and kissed him on the cheek at the same time putting her arms around his neck. He felt his heart racing now more than ever. Here they were, complete strangers, embraced in the middle of the bog.

"Thanks for being so kind to me." she whispered.

"It was my pleasure." replied Michael.

With that she gave him a gentle kiss on the cheek affectionately like a sister kissing a brother. The sound of the train whistle in the distance signalled dinner time for Michael.

"Well, I had better be making my way now," said Sally. "John will be wondering what has happened."

"Look you might as well come with me now," said Michael "that is the quickest way back to the main road."

Sally agreed and both set off for his home, which was about a mile distant down the rough cart track.

"Now you'll stay for some dinner and Michael will give you a lift into town," insisted Mrs. Corcoran, eager to make her unexpected guest welcome.

"You are very kind, Mrs. Corcoran." replied Sally.

"I'll bet you have a good appetite me girl after your long walk?"

"Yes I have - it must be the fresh air."

Mrs. Corcoran produced a wholesome meal of jacket potatoes, fresh green cabbage, swede and some or Moran's best lean bacon, which was enjoyed by all. Needless to say there was nothing left on the plates when they had finished. After Sally had helped with the washing-up and they had chatted over a cup of Mrs. Corcoran's tea it was time to go - she was already late. Sally thanked Mrs. Corcoran for her generous hospitality and apologised for having to leave so soon afterwards.

"He is a bit of a dark horse you know," joked Mrs. Corcoran.

"He never told me he was inviting a pretty girl to dinner."

Sally smiled and looked at Michael.

"Your son has been very kind to me, Mrs. Corcoran. I can see he takes after his mother."

"It's time now he was thinking about settling down," said his mother at the same time giving a wink of her eye. Sally smiled.

Michael wished his mother hadn't said that. It just caused all his old fears to come rushing back again. Sally sensed his unease too. It was just his luck that she was off now to meet someone else.

"Why are all the nice girls spoken for?" he asked himself.

"I'll drive you into town now," interrupted Michael "otherwise you'll be late for your appointment."

"Yes, and I did promise John I would be back early - we have arranged to see Father Flynn this afternoon."

The words echoed in Michael's mind as he started the car while Sally and his mother said goodbye. He could picture her and John walking up the aisle. She would make a pretty bride he thought to himself. Still it was nice meeting Sally and he wished her well in the future.

"John, whoever he is, is a lucky man," he thought "and perhaps those town girls are not so bad after all."

For a moment he was again lost in his own thoughts.

"Michael! Michael!" his mother called.

"Yes Mother".

"Sally wants to know if it would be alright for her to help out with the turf on Saturday?"

He recognised the mischievous twinkle in his mother's eye.

"That will be great - I could do with the extra help. It should be in good condition by then if the weather keeps up."

"I would love to help," added Sally "and perhaps John could come along too and give a hand?"

"Why not, indeed?" said Mrs. Corcoran.

"Oh incidentally," said Sally, "did I mention that my brother John was a priest? He's home on holiday for a few weeks."

"No ....no, you didn't." answered Michael, trying to hide his feeling of relief.

Somehow, he had a feeling that working on the bog would never be quite the same again.

"I'm sure now I can find a job for him to do." laughed Michael.

The Chicken Farmer's Wife

The slightly stooped figure of Percy Clapworthy was a familiar sight amongst the River Valley Allotment holders. Regular as clockwork, and complete with rucksack, he could be seen making his way through the earthen patchwork.

"Good morning, Percy." greeted old Mulvaney.

"Mornin'." grunted Percy as he continued on his way muttering to himself.

He was a grumpy individual who could hardly bring himself to pass the time of day. Percy Clapworthy wore a dirty old mackintosh and cloth cap with the peak pointing backwards. He looked all of his fifty odd years as he pushed his bicycle along the grass pathway.

Percy had succeeded in building a small two-wheel contraption, which he hitched to the saddle bar of the bicycle. By this means he transported the season's produce, such as it was. More importantly, he used it to bring food for his chickens. To other members he was known simply as the Chicken Farmer because this was his principal interest.

If Percy Clapworthy was a rather reserved man his wife was the very opposite? Not, of course, that she was often seen down at the allotments. Some of the allotment folk felt sorry for Percy and reckoned he must have a terrible life with the woman.

She was about the same age as Percy and a lady of generous proportions. Her face was as hard as hobnail boots with a square mouth. She wore a bright floral dress, which reached a point halfway between her knees and ankles. If her appearance was threatening enough, it was nothing compared with her tongue.

In between the novenas and the nagging, life was far from peaceful for Percy. It was common knowledge that he had taken up 'chicken farming' just to get away from the woman. Rumour had it that she often used violence against her husband. On one occasion he returned late after 'Loopy' Larkin was taken to the church. She greeted him at the front door and chased the poor fellow around the garden wielding a brass candlestick. If he did venture out at night, she would want to know exactly where he had been and whose company he was in.

Mind you, to see her walking up the church in her Sunday best she was the picture of sainthood in the making. It was hard to imagine that a cross word could ever pass her lips. If the marriage had not turned out very well, the writing was on the wall from the start. Well, who ever heard of a woman taking a statue of the Blessed Virgin to bed on her wedding night?

After all those years, Percy Clapworthy was reconciled to his plight. By spending as little time as possible around the house he avoided confrontation. When he was not at work he would take refuge in the allotment tending his chickens.

Their chattering made a refreshing change from his wife's persistent nagging. Sometimes he thought the chickens understood him and his problems. On the rare occasions that she did visit looking for eggs there was a noticeable change in their temperament.

"Chickens can sense these things," he

would mutter to himself.

To be fair things had mellowed a little between them with the passing years. He had his life - such as it was - and she had her's. A certain dependence on each other had kept them together. She maintained the house and he provided the money at the end of each month.

Percy Clapworthy and his wife would be married twenty-five years next month. He was determined, despite their ups and downs, that the occasion should not go unmarked. Percy had planned a celebration, which was to be a surprise. Friends and neighbours were invited and sworn to secrecy. The venue was to be the local public house.

He was not noted for his propensity to spend his 'hard earned money'. Some of the neighbours quietly questioned the man's sanity. On the other hand, twenty-five years of marriage was no mean achievement.

Imagine the shock when he revealed, quite by chance, that she had " up'd and away " after all those years. While he had been busy planning the event, and scraping to find the money to pay for it all, she had been preparing to go off with some good-for-nothing so and so of a toy boy half her age. The whole place was aghast. Percy had certainly won the sympathy vote.

It shouldn't really have come as such a shock when all was said and done. The greatest surprise for the neighbours was that the like of her found someone daft enough to take her in toe. The news had yet to reach the allotment where life continued at its usual snails' pace.

"It won't be long now, Percy, 'till the big occasion," said Mulvaney.

"There'll be no big occasion or small one for that matter," retorted the Chicken Farmer.

"And why is that now?"

"God Blast her! Hasn't she gone and left me."

There was an embarrassing silence over the place and you could almost hear the greenfly chewing the cud. Mulvaney was lost for words and promptly resumed his hoeing.

"Gone off with some young fellow," added Percy "and good riddance, that's all I say."

The talking point of the whole locality - not to mention River Valley Allotments - was the Chicken Farmer's wife. Despite his misfortune, the Chicken Farmer would come every evening to tend and feed his chickens. His visits were more frequent now. Some days he would come morning and evening.

Apart from his chickens, like all other allotment folk, Percy Clapworthy's work and routine were dictated by the seasons and the weather. Digging over the patch in autumn, sowing and planting in spring and the endless hoeing and weeding.

Chickens were different. They had to be fed and watered regularly. You couldn't leave them for months and simply forget about them. The Chicken Farmer had not bothered very much about vegetables in the past - just some cabbage, carrots and onions mainly.

This year it was different. Percy would be seen with his jacket off and shirtsleeves rolled up digging away late into the evening.

"I fancy some nice runner beans this year." said the Chicken Farmer one day when one of the more inquisitive members asked about the big trench he was digging.

"You can't beat runner beans. Maybe I'll sow some tatties too." added Percy.

By now he had almost finished a new henhouse. Soon he would be able to increase his stock. After all he would have more time now for looking after them.

One morning Mulvaney noticed that there was a flurry of activity above in Percy Clapworthy's allotment. For a while he thought Percy had got some help with people digging and wheeling barrow loads of soil back and forth. It all proved too much for Mulvaney who could not resist a closer look.

"I'm sorry, Sir, this area is sealed off," said the policeman.

The slightly bent figure of the Chicken Farmer being led away was a forlorn sight.

The police never did find the body of Mrs.Clapworthy and she was never seen or heard of again. The jury returned a verdict of 'not guilty' to the charge of murder. The case made the front page of the local press.

"CHICKEN FARMER ACQUITTED OF WIFE'S MURDER," read the headline

That year Percy Clapworthy won first prize for the best pair of birds in the local show. The judge said he had never seen such well-nourished specimens in all his years of judging. The Chicken Farmer smiled quietly to himself.

The Canal Walker

As Michael Galvin walked along the frozen Grand Union Canal on a cold winter's morning there was a sense of enchantment in the air. The towpath was crisp after a good night's frost and the ducks and water hens stepped lightly on the patterned ice sheet now joining the two banks. The smell of burning logs from the narrow boats reminded him of Ireland. For a time, Michael Galvin was back there, walking along the banks of the River Lung.

One of his favourite pastimes in those early years was fishing on the River Lung. The Lung Valley was an angler's paradise and had some of the best coarse fishing waters in Ireland for bream, roach, rudd, perch, tench, eel, pike and trout.

The canal was a peaceful, tranquil place where Michael could be alone with his thoughts. It had the ability, in his mind at least, to transport him to those familiar haunts of his youth. Butter cups, daises, purple clover and meadow sweet, growing on the grassy path, were poignant reminders of Irish meadow fields and a carefree time long past.

The Irish seasons were mirrored in the hedgerows that hid the canal from the wider, harsher and less welcoming world - hawthorn and blackthorn blossom, hazel and holly. The slow pace of life on the canal was a reminder of an Ireland that had almost disappeared although some vestiges of this way of life could still be found if you searched hard enough.

The River Lung flows into Lough Gara, on

the border of Counties Sligo and Roscommon, where Michael spent much of his youth. In his mind's eye he could still see the remains of the ancient crannogs along its shoreline and the Greenland Geese that chose to spend their winters there and graze on adjacent grasslands. They too were at home in this place, at least for the winter months.

The old cottage, with its white walls and black corrugated iron roof, had stood there for at least two hundred years, amidst the small stone-walled fields and tall hedges, just a short distance from the lake. This traditional stone building with its small windows and irregular walls was his escape, even if his visits were just a couple of times a year. It was not the time spent in this old and often cold cottage or working in the garden that was important. His roots were in the place and the memories and images accumulated would sustain him in the months ahead.

As he continued along the canal, past the remains of dead embers, Michael could picture the large open fireplace and almost feel the heat from the turf fire. The cottage was situated within a few feet of the lane with a stone-paved 'street' to the front. All the old houses had a street where the hens would be found when they were not raiding the hedges, the fields, the flower and vegetable gardens, leaving their footprints, feathers and the rest wherever they went.

The true traditional Irish house was built of compacted mud but few of these old buildings survive today. Mud cabins have been around for thousands of years. At the time of the Famine in the 1840's it is estimated that at least four million people lived in mud houses in Ireland.

These older houses, built from local materials such as clay, stone, timber gathered from the bogs and thatch harvested from the fields were in harmony with their surroundings. Building such humble dwellings was a community effort. There were no plans other than those in the builders' head and local styles evolved. The small windows were wider on the inside to allow more light into the house. The half-door served a similar purpose and also kept the foul out of the kitchen.

"You don't see many thatched houses as you walk along the canal," Michael pondered to himself. Still, it took him into the heart of the countryside … and beyond – to the byways and fields of Sligo.

Many people were not sorry to see thatch go. Chaff falling down between the ceiling boards created dust. The sight of straw pieces blowing around the yard made the place untidy. For many owners, maintaining a thatched roof was simply too much trouble and expense.

For some, it represented a cosy past invoking an image of a thatched cottage nestling snugly into the landscape with a wisp of white smoke rising towards the sky. For others, it evoked a very different story – one of poverty, hunger and deprivation – a past they wanted to leave behind. Today, the thatched dwelling has been relegated to the postcard, porcelain replicas and cheap souvenirs in airport departure lounges.

The houses along the Grand Union Canal were different and much sought after in residential areas.

There was something mysterious and magical about Lough Gara and its ancient crannogs. This remote and beautiful lake seemed to invite and at the same time repel the casual visitor. It has a number of natural islands: Inch Island, Crow Island, Eagles Island and summertime peninsulas that become islands in the winter – Inchmore, Derrymore Island and Emlagh. The Annals of the Four Masters record that in 1435 an O'Gara was slain by his kinsmen on an island in Lough Gara, which was formerly known as Loch Techet.

St. Attracta, who was born in the 5th Century, founded a convent and hospice for travellers where the seven roads met at Killaraght near Lough Gara, which still existed as late as 1539. She was a contemporary of St. Patrick from whom she received the veil.

He had allowed his mind to wander too much. It was time to return to the present – time to leave those memories behind, at least for the now.

As he rounded a bend, Michael Galvin stared at the large grey two-story house on the canal side, which bore the year it was built – 1916 - the year of Ireland's Easter Rising……

Hogan's Gap

It was my wife who suggested that I take the children away for a week and rent a cottage in Ireland. Initially, the idea of a winter holiday in the country did not appeal to me. I had not been to Ireland since my army days in the early seventies.

The chap in the local shop was helpful if a little surprised that anyone should ask directions for "Hill Top Cottage".

"Keep going up the hill until you cross the stream by the old Mill and then turn left just before Hogan's Gap."

The narrow road wound its way through the trees, which at times blocked out the sunlight creating an eerie shadowy effect. The overnight fall of snow was now starting to clear. The countryside looked quite breathtaking. The snowcapped mountains, with their abundance of fir trees, gave the place a crisp freshness and beauty. The incline was now quite steep. Already, we were looking down across the small stone-walled enclosures towards the graveyard. The ruined church stood out clearly, perched as it was, on the hill. Further below was Lough Shee.

It was a typically Irish cottage with a neatly thatched roof and freshly whitewashed walls - so unlike those Belfast terraced houses with their neat gardens, screaming children and weeping widows. Quickly, I dismissed those memories from my mind. Yet, there was something strange about the place. The contrast with suburban London too could hardly have been more marked. The sounds of the nearby waterfall and the groaning of the ice on Lough Shee as it creaked and cracked with the thaw had replaced the noise of the traffic.

The next morning, I remember waking up in a cold sweat and feeling totally disoriented. Once again, I was back on the streets of Belfast. A sniper's shot rang out. Browne was lying in a pool of blood in the gutter - shot through the head. His funeral was a mournful sight as his two young children grasped their mother's coat in the wind and rain. That was a long time ago now - time to forget but the memory was too clearly etched on my mind ever to be forgotten. Outside, it was starting to get light. Suddenly, the room door burst open and in came Clare, followed by John.

"Come quickly, Daddy, quickly," she shouted excitedly.

She was out of breath and obviously very distressed.

"I saw a strange man. Daddy, I really did," added John.

"Now calm down the two of you." I said.

"We saw him. Daddy …we did … staring in the front bedroom window and smiling and ...and being just frightening and horrible."

I searched around the house with the aid of an old bicycle lamp but failed to find any intruder or peeping Tom or Pat for that matter. Nevertheless, the two children remained emphatic sticking to their story of the man with the smiling face and staring eyes.

"Ah that was old McGONIGLE. He's a little bit simple - one sod short of a load of turf you might say," said MORAN, the landlord of the local pub.

"Well his behaviour was certainly strange." I replied.

96

The children had been right.

"Best Gaelic footballer in the County in his day," said the landlord, "then, instead of the ball, he caught one of them German bombs somewhere out foreign."

The next night there was no mistaking what woke me up in the middle of the night. For a few seconds, I lay there, half asleep and half awake, listening to the sounds. Desperately, I strained my ears in an effort to distinguish the words spoken by the strange voices, which came from the living room, interspersed with bursts of laughter. Underneath the door I could see the living room light.

Eventually, the voices grew silent and I drifted into a deep sleep. I woke up some time later to hear marching footsteps in the distance.

"Tramp! Tramp! Tramp!"

The deafening and monotonous sound made by the heavy boots against the hard roadway grew louder and louder. I held my breath. My travel alarm showed the time to be 3.00am.

"Tramp! Tramp! Tramp!"

The footsteps were much closer now. Before I could summon enough courage to look out of the room window - never mind see if the children were still asleep - a voice yelled out.

"Halt!" The marching troop came to a stand outside.

"Fire!" came the order and immediately a volley of shots rang out followed by shouting and screaming. It was as if all Hell had erupted at that very moment.

I cannot remember just how long this commotion lasted. It was probably no more than a few minutes but seemed much longer.

Fortunately, Clare and John had slept through the uproar. Eventually, the shooting and the shouting ended. The sound of voices was heard again. Now, the laughter had changed to pitiful crying and sobbing with the occasional painful moan.

Once more, I listened intently, trying to work out what was happening and - more to the point - what might happen to the children and myself. It was then that I heard a voice speak.

"I hope you'll forgive us for intruding, Mr.Conroy, but it's a cold night outside."

I turned around to see the figures of two men sitting by the fire. I recognised the blood stained British Army officer's uniform worn by the man who had spoken. The second man carried a revolver in a holster and wore the dress of an Irish Freedom Fighter.

"You must have been in a deep sleep - the sleep of the dead surely." said the freedom fighter.

"Who are you - what are you doing here?" I demanded.

"Call me Hogan. Sit down Mr. Conroy."

"I want to know what you are doing in my place?"

"This is not your place. It's no one's place," said Hogan.

"It belongs to those who are long dead - gone - forgotten. Fair winds carry their spirits through the uplands and lowlands of Ireland."

"We're all dead ... dead ...dead and forgotten," added the soldier.

"I don't understand," I said, growing more impatient and apprehensive.

"No one understands the power, the force, that drives a man to seek his freedom; to realise his nations dreams; unshackle the chains that bind him - and then, to be damned," continued Hogan.

"Or another man who seeks to deny him those dreams," said the soldier.

By now it was obvious that they were no longer speaking to me and even appeared oblivious to my presence. I felt decidedly uncomfortable and just wanted to grab my two sleeping children and run ... and run, as fast as I could. Was I really listening to a conversation between two men who had at some time in the distant past lost their lives fighting for Ireland?

"No one understands the futility of a lost life, gone but for the blood spilt on the dusty roads of Ireland," said the freedom fighter.

"I served my queen and my country and I cursed the traitors whose cause I despised - and never understood - and now I am dead."

"And I too am dead - cut down in the struggle."

"That was a long time ago," added the soldier.

"A very long time ago."

"A few of the others survived the ambush."

"Just a few ... just a few survivors on both sides."

"And still the killing goes on ... and on ... and on ... like the waves lapping on the shores of Lough Shee below," continued Hogan.

"And what has it all achieved? All the killing, all the hatred, all the grieving?" asked the soldier, burying his face in his hands.

Suddenly, the freedom fighter stood up.

"Why don't they listen to us, the voices

of the dead? Can they not hear us calling in the dark, dark night ... calling ... calling."

Someone banging on the front door interrupted the conversation.

"Knock! Knock! Knock!"

I rushed to the children's room to find Clare and John sitting up in bed crying.

"It's alright - everything is alright," I tried to reassure them.

"I can't get to sleep with all the noise," sobbed Clare.

"Please sleep in our room, Daddy," pleaded John, as I tucked them in once more.

The front door slammed shut which seemed to make the whole house shake. I glanced out of the bedroom window just in time to see the undertakers in their dark suits and tall hats place the two coffins in horse drawn carriages. The two strange visitors had gone. Everything seemed peaceful again. The children slept...

"Are we really going to stay in a bed and breakfast house next time?" asked Clare, enthusiastically.

"Yes, of course we are - no more rented cottages - at least not in these parts."

The Retirement Party

Dennis O'Connor was oblivious to the whispered conversations, which filled the room like the smoke from the cheap cigars. He was in a world of his own. He had been a policeman in London for thirty years rising to the rank of inspector.

Old friends and colleagues had gathered to say farewell. Many of the younger officers were there too. He was well regarded by all. The police service had been good to him over the years. The money had been poor in the early years when the children were small. If it hadn't been for the drunks he wheeled into the police station at the end of a late shift, and the bit of overtime for Court in the morning, they might have starved. Of course, all that has changed now with new court procedures and new legislation.

He was a quiet, unassuming, man but tonight he was the main focus of attention. The others crowded around him and reminisced about the old days and their mutual exploits. In overheard conversations around the room you could hear:

"O'Connor could smell a thief five miles away."

"He was a good practical copper." "One of the old school." "The Guv'nor will be missed."

And so it went on - tonight was Dennis O'Connor's special night.

He looked very smart in his navy pin striped suit with matching tie and handkerchief. His grey hair was neatly combed and parted as usual. Tonight, he had a sense of presence although normally he kept a rather low profile.

O'Connor had achieved the rank of Inspector by his own hard efforts and the support of some fine colleagues. Being in the right place at the right time had also helped. Many a good arrest had been made by a policeman who should have been somewhere else.

There was the time as a young constable on the beat that he had tried to snatch a few hours' sleep on nights only to be disturbed by a burglar. He received a commendation from the Chief Constable for good police work in making an excellent arrest, which cleared up a particularly nasty series of burglaries in the area.

On other occasions he hadn't been quite so lucky. There was the time he borrowed a police car to tow his caravan on holiday. No one would have noticed, perhaps, if the children had not been singing and shouting and dangling their sand buckets and spades out of the back windows of the police car. He was disciplined and fined a week's pay.

Dennis O'Connor had never been greedy for promotion and had been overtaken by many of his younger colleagues. He knew his own capabilities much better than any promotion board. He harboured no resentment but wondered, sometimes, about some of the recent promotions.

If he had been prepared to move around the Force more often he would probably have reached the rank of Superintendent. Then everything has a price and his family was more important.

He had seen the pressures and stresses which existed between the 'job' and an officer's family life. All too often the strain proved too great leading to the break-up of a marriage and children left without a father. The police service demands a great deal from an officer and his family.

Occasionally, it was the officers themselves who placed personal ambition, the excitement of the job and the comradeship of colleagues, before family life. Sometimes, he had seen officers loose both family and job.

The party was well under way now. People moved around the room weaving their way through the various groups deep in conversation. The clinking of glasses and popping of corks could now be heard above the now louder hum of the crowd.

It was important to be seen rubbing shoulders with a few well-placed senior officers on these occasions - or so the more ambitious seemed to think. It could mean the difference between success and failure on a promotion board. Indeed, there were a few present that had an eye on O'Connor's job. Anyway, one or two friends in the right place were always useful if only to get you out of trouble.

In the old days all you needed to be promoted was to be a good thief taker. In his day, Dennis O'Connor had felt more collars than some of the young ones today had hot dinners.

Mind you, there was a different sort of villain in those days - good villains. You couldn't help respecting them. It's different today - guns and drugs and hooligans. When O'Connor was a young copper on the beat a pickpocket was a real professional. They worked as a team and each had his own part. The poor victim didn't even know he had been 'dipped'. Now, however, it was a knife through the heart for a few pounds.

Of course, the job was different now - full of young whiz kids straight from university and wet behind the ears. What do they know about life? It is all social awareness training now - nothing to do with catching villains. Down at the Force Training Centre all they seem to talk about is NVC's - nonverbal communication as they call it.

Nowadays, you needed to be more than just a good policeman. The job was different - or was it really? Dennis O'Connor found it difficult to understand how three years at some university studying social anthropology - all expenses paid - made you a better copper. It followed, of course, that if the Force spends that amount of money on you then you must be worthy of promotion.

"Well, the Chief Constable has to justify his annual budget and expenditure, hasn't he?"

But then O'Connor was one of the old style policemen. It was time to retire, all right.

Many of the old hands from the job had come along for a final drink with the guv'nor. They were now almost a thing of the past. They had grown up with the Force and worked their way up the ranks - sergeant, inspector, and superintendent. They were a mixed bunch all right, some certainly more colourful than others. One or two sailed a bit close to the wind in their time. But then as the sceptic would say,

"The open prisons are full of policemen, solicitors and accountants." Insider dealers, politicians and bankers could also be added to the list.

There were others who, unfortunately, succumbed to the evil of drink due no doubt to the pressures of the job or so they would have us believe. Then, of course, there were the womanisers. Old Philpot had a novel way of finding an excuse to spend time with his lady friend. He would type out a memorandum from the superintendent, addressed to himself instructing him to attend a training course.

A copy of the document would then be placed in his inside breast pocket where his wife was sure to look. Since they didn't talk to each other she never queried the number of courses he attended in a given year! It was only when she rang the police station to find out if he was still on the course that she found out that he had retired six weeks earlier.

A few more robust characters managed to combine all three leanings - and still live to draw the police pension. Most officers, however, were hardworking and dedicated. They took pride in their work and regularly risked their lives for the community they served.

He would miss them all - each a character partly shaped by years spent dealing with the dross of life. Now Dennis O'Connor would have time on his hands. There would be no need to get up at 4.30am to catch the train for early turn. He would no longer have to make the daily journey to and from London.

When P.C.Luckless died on a train on his way home from work no one noticed - they thought he was asleep. Eventually, the train carried his body back to London again.

Strange, isn't it - travelling to work when you're dead.

Life would go on as usual when he had gone. Children would be abducted and molested by perverted men, women raped and old people battered around the head and left for dead for the price of a quick fix.

"Dennis O'Connor has given the Force thirty years of loyal, dedicated service. He has been an example and an inspiration to all officers with whom he worked and will be remembered for many years to come." said the Chief Constable.

Dennis appeared indifferent to the words spoken.

"Would he … be remembered?"

"Remember old 'what's his name'?" Yes, that was more like it.

It was always the same. Only when someone was transferred or retired were they told that they had done a good job. So much for non-verbal communication and inter-personal skills. A little recognition at the time would be nice occasionally.

"Of course, we must also thank Mrs. O'Connor and the whole family for supporting Dennis over the years."

Dennis O'Connor wasn't listening. The words of thanks fell on deaf ears.

He was certainly looking much more relaxed now - gone was the furrowed brow and high colour, which represented a lifetime of work and responsibility. Colleagues and friends wished their host well for the future. It had been a good party - the empty glasses and filled ash trays were evidence enough of that. He had certainly enjoyed it.

Dennis O'Connor smiled quietly to himself as he gently drew back the heavenly curtain

for one final look as the men in dark suits
placed the heavy lid on his coffin.
  What's his name had finally retired.

A Tramp

When Flannagan walked out the door all those summers ago he had said goodbye to everything that was important in his life. The children were too young to understand but old enough never to forget. True, he had taken the cowardly way out - he knew that, as did everybody else. Now he must live with the shame of it in the same way that they had to live without a father to hold them on his knee or read a bedtime story.

He huddled up in a dark corner of the railway station trying to keep warm. Years spent travelling the country with no proper place to lay his head and little food in his stomach had left him soul-weary - a ragged figure, broken in body and spirit. London did not appear to hold out any more promise than any of the other big cities and towns he had visited in his time.

Flannagan was unshaven, a man in his fifties now, tall and slightly stooped. He walked with a limp and wore scraggy trousers and an ill-fitting old overcoat.

"All right Flannagan, on your way now." called the policeman.

"Just, just going, sir." he replied touching his old tattered cloth cap at the same time.

"Well he has a job to do, I suppose." thought Flannagan, who had more than his fair share of encounters with the law although nothing too serious. Anyhow, his type was not encouraged at the station these times.

Victoria Railway Station was certainly

much brighter now but he knew that it would take more than a fresh coat of paint and a few artificial flowers to conceal the evils which pervaded the place.

"When you're homeless like me," he pondered, "you see the seedier side of life - from rent boys to racketeers; from pimps to pushers."

Flannagan knew only too well that the dregs of humanity could be seen there and now he had become part of that unsavoury scene.

He had worked hard and played hard too as he travelled the length and breadth of Britain seeking work wherever it was to be found and the good money that went with it. Like so many others, he paid scant regard to the future and old age. It was as if he continually needed to dull his memories and regrets in case they became too painful to bear. All that was a long time ago now.

Flannagan turned up the collar of his coat, straightened his cap and braced himself to face the elements. He longed for a decent meal and was sick of rummaging in waste bins looking for other people's leavings. For him, the fast-food revolution was not take-a-ways but the throw-a-ways on which he so frequently depended for his next bite.

The station was noisy with the ceaseless hustle and bustle of people coming and going. The clanging of railway cages being drawn across the concourse was deafening.

Slowly, shoulders stooped, he made his way across the piazza outside the nearby Westminster Cathedral. People hurried back and forth, umbrellas raised, and he could feel the rain and hail beating against his face. He felt the water penetrate the holes in his shoes and his feet were cold as ice. For a brief moment he hesitated to admire the magnificent building, which towered high above him.

"Can't remember when I last stood in a church," he thought to himself.

He had lost that too - his religion. Mind you he had often wanted to go to Mass or Confessions but "What's the point," he felt "after so many years?".

"If the Almighty keeps an attendance register then surely my name must have been crossed out long ago."

His mind wandered back to the little church on the hill in the west of Ireland where he served Mass as a child. He was feeling sad again as he thought of the home and family he had left behind all those years ago. The passing of the years had not wiped away the memories. Instead, somehow they were all the more poignant now - eating away at his very being. Tears dimmed his eyes and his heart was heavy.

While the old man stood there in the rain gazing up at the imposing Cathedral he heard a little voice calling:

"Would you like to shelter under my umbrella, Mister?" said the small girl in an unmistakable soft Irish accent.

"That's, that's very kind of you," said Flannagan in a faltering voice, touched by the child's gesture.

He bent down to thank the little girl who could hardly have been more than six. She was now staring him in the face with her large blue eyes and warm smile, which he could feel tugging at his heartstrings mercilessly. Just for one fleeting moment he thought he recognised the little face and head of blond curls. Yes, she reminded him of his own daughter but then that was twenty-five years ago and a lot of water had flowed under London Bridge in that time.

"Come on, Katie," snapped her anxious mother "I told you not to wander off and don't talk to strangers." The little girl ran off after her mother occasionally glancing behind. Flannagan watched, drew a deep breath and sighed quietly to himself.

He was feeling tired now and the rain was getting much heavier. Flannagan looked towards the open Cathedral door, hesitated, and then slowly started to walk up the steps taking hold of the wall for support.

Inside, a new world seemed to open up before him. He took off his cap and stood for a moment admiring the vast interior with its great marble columns and high painted ceiling. A choir sung to the accompaniment of the great organ, the sound of which resounded throughout the building. The smell of incense filled the place. A bishop and several priests were concelebrating High Mass.

Once more, the memories came flooding back to him as he watched the drops fall from his coat onto the shiny waxed floor which was pitted from years of wear and prayer. Flannagan felt a pathetic creature standing at the back of the Cathedral drenched to the skin. He felt the shivers in his back and his hands trembled. He longed for the sight of a friendly face among the crowds; the touch of a warm hand; the familiar sound of his own name. His was a pitiful existence. He had lost his sense of dignity long ago.

Occasionally, during his more lucid

moments, the stench of stale beer and tobacco would give way to the more pleasant smells he associated with Ireland: the smell of heather burning on a hillside in the still evening air; newly cut meadow after a day's warm sun; the smell of freshly cut turf straight from the slain.

Although these existed only in his mind they were real enough to him and never failed to carry him on a mental journey back home. Even with the passing of so many years Flannagan still cherished the old place as home.

There was a feeling of tranquility now. Somehow, at that moment he felt close to God - closer than he had felt for many years. Here he was, part of the congregation at the Mass and all he came in for was shelter from the rain and the cold wind - and, yes, he thought "shelter too from the cruel world outside."

The image of the little girl in the rain seemed to keep appearing before his eyes haunting him. The warmth and love in her face reminded him that he was still human; someone who had feelings; someone who needed the love of other people. At least one little girl thought that. Despite the dirty old clothes, the worn shoes and the many all too recognisable signs of years travelling the roads, there was still something there, which stirred deep within his soul.

"I'll go to confessions." he murmured to himself, avoiding the disapproving glances of the tourists as they strolled around. He felt confused and afraid.

"But what will the priest think of me after all those years and the life I have had?" he thought.

Now, he felt torn apart. Yet something forced him to join the queue of people waiting for Mass to finish and confessions to start.

"There's no turning back now," he thought as he desperately tried to remember the words of the Confiteor and wondered about the priest's reaction.

"Twenty years since my last Confession, Father - twenty years." It sounded like an eternity.

The Mass was drawing to a close now and Flannagan could feel his heart racing as the Cathedral Choir sang "Faith of Our Fathers" and the bishop, priests and servers began to leave the alter. The sound of the organ was intense now and filled the Cathedral. Slowly, the solemn procession made its way down the centre aisle.

Then, unexpectedly, the procession turned sharp left and headed straight for where Flannagan was kneeling. He felt an irresistible impulse to leave, to get as far away from the place as possible but felt trapped again. It was as if he was dead and yet, somehow, partaking in his own Requiem Mass and now the bishop and priests were about to bless his coffin. A feeling of sheer panic and helplessness flowed through his whole body and he failed to notice that the grand procession had now turned left again as it made its way to the sacristy and away from the Confessional.

The place was quiet again and the young priest listened as Flannagan told his story. In the intimacy of the confessional box it was as though his past and present had been brought face to face – and, somehow, he felt better.

There was a spring in his step as he made his way to the exit. It was as if a great load had somehow been lifted off his shoulders. The priest had given him some sound advice and, somehow, he thought that things might, just might, change. Flannagan had learned the meaning of hope again and he remembered the priest's kind softly spoken invitation.

"Call at the Presbytery at five o'clock and there will be a hot meal waiting for you."

"I must not be late," he thought as his empty stomach started to rumble again with the thought of food.

Nervously, Flannagan knocked on the door of the Presbytery as the clock struck five. First, he knocked lightly and then a heavier knock. This time the door was opened and immediately he recognised the little girl with the large blue eyes, penetrating smile and head of curls. Could it be that he had called at the wrong house, he wondered.

"I'm ... I'm sorry I thought..."

The appearance of the tall figure of the young priest interrupted his faltering apology. After a warm handshake he was ushered into the front room where the little girl's mother was seated.

"Welcome home Dad, it's been a long time." she said at the same time throwing her arms around him and giving him a close hug.

He tried hard to fight back the tears, which welled up in his eyes but they just flowed. Her years of searching had finally been rewarded.

"I knew I had a granddad, Mammy, I really did." said the young girl excitedly.

Through his tears the old man was

beginning to see things a little more
clearly now.

Night Rider

Jane just managed to join the Holyhead train as the guard gave a final blast on his whistle. Breathing a sigh of relief she rested before finding a seat.

"Mum and Dad would be very disappointed if I wasn't on the Dublin train tomorrow," she thought to herself.

She didn't really like travelling in mid-January but this was a special visit. A feeling of excitement rushed through her body as she looked forward to the big reunion of family, relations and friends.

"Well twenty-five years of marriage is well worth celebrating," she thought.

The rain hammered away at the windows as the train left the lights and shelter of Euston Station. It seemed so dark outside. The train rocked to and fro making it difficult to maintain balance as it gradually gained speed.

The train was not very crowded and her coach was virtually empty. Jane began to feel very much alone. For a moment she wished she hadn't been on duty over the Christmas period. Christmas would have been a much nicer time to go home. She scarcely noticed the middle aged gentleman, who was to share her compartment until she tripped on his foot as she struggled with her luggage,

"I'm very sorry. Oh how clumsy of me." she said most apologetically.

She looked around the compartment, which was rather drab with torn curtains and a light, which seemed to flicker between very dim and very bright. The rain continued to beat endlessly on the window. Her eyes rested on the headline of the London Evening Standard, which her travelling companion was reading. In large black letters were the words

"LONDON KILLER STRIKES AGAIN."

The man took a drink from a can of beer and continued to read his paper. He didn't seem to notice that she was staring.

Jane felt a little uncomfortable. Strange thoughts drifted through her mind. Quickly she dismissed her fears and started to read her book. It would have been nice if there was at least one more person, in the compartment.

Her concentration was broken by the sound of a wasp on the window ledge. She realised that the other person in her compartment was becoming angry, striking out at the wasp with his folded newspaper. She watched as the wasp continued to move around the glass, somehow managing to evade his blows. The male passenger was now playing a sadistic game with the wasp while at the same time trying to attract Jane's attention. She began to feel upset.

"Why can't he just kill it?" she thought.

She didn't like the thought of the wasp suffering.

Her polite smile in response to the strangers obvious staring concealed her real fear. She felt decidedly uneasy about the man's behaviour. There is something not quite right about him but she couldn't put her finger on it.

'Can't stand bloody wasps, detest them!" he growled.

By now he was really tantalising the creature.

"Oh! neither can I," she replied timidly, "Would you mind killing it - wasps can be very dangerous."

"Kill it! kill it! No, that's too easy. It's my prisoner, I can do what I like with it. It's completely at my mercy."

Jane felt afraid and was sorry she spoke. Suddenly, she too felt like a prisoner.

"Calm down, relax," she said to herself.

Perhaps it was the drink, which made him behave in this peculiar manner. She tried reading her book again but could not concentrate. Something caused her to glance up at the luggage rack. She noticed the bulky holdall with a damp patch on the bottom. Her heart skipped a beat when she noticed blood dripping on to the light shade immediately behind her fellow traveller.

A cold shiver ran down her spine and she felt as though she was going to be sick. The newspaper headline passed before her mind again:

"LONDON KILLER STRIKES AGAIN".

Her first thought was to move to another compartment. However, this might attract attention. Jane decided to remain where she was.

"Maybe I should pull the communication cord," she thought as her heart raced and she wondered if, in fact, he could hear it beating.

On reflection, that, too, was not a good idea. He might direct his anger at her. Who knows what he might do?

"What has he already done?" she wondered, glancing again at the holdall and the dripping blood.

She felt trapped and helpless.

He had just started to sleep when the

train suddenly came to a halt. She looked out the window staring into the blackness of night through the rain-spattered windows; there was a deathly silence. The train had stopped miles from anywhere.

The sudden jerk of the train stopping caused him to wake up.

"Why have we stopped here in the middle of bloody nowhere?" he demanded to know.

Jane shook her head suggesting that, perhaps, it was a red signal.

"There's always some excuse - always some bloody excuse."

He was now very aggressive. There were spatters of blood on his white shirt but he hadn't noticed them - not yet.

He continued to mutter to himself and Jane pretended not to notice. Suddenly, the guard came along the corridor calling out:

"There's been a point's failure. Hopefully, we can get it sorted out fairly quickly."

She attempted to speak to the guard but somehow couldn't find the words in time. Her companion was now looking at her with a fixed stare. She felt his eyes penetrating deep into her mind. It seemed as though there were only the two of them alone on the train in the middle of the night, miles from civilisation.

There was a sudden jerk and the train started to move on again. Without warning, the man produced a knife, which he held in an admiring and menacing way. A feeling of terror ran through her blood as their eyes met. Any attempt to pull the communication cord at this stage could result in a violent attack on her. Sue was shaking and felt cold and sick.

"I think I'm going to enjoy this journey." he said in a sinister and intimidating, voice."

"Please, please - put that knife away. I can't stand knives," Jane pleaded.

"I can do just what I want on this train. There's just you and me - how cosy."

"Oh please, I beg you, leave me alone."

"Shall we play a little game like we did with the wasp?" the man said, teasingly.

She felt desperate and helpless in a way, which she had never experienced before.

"This man is capable of anything," she thought to herself.

He could, simply throw her out of the train and no one would suspect anything but an accident. She screamed with panic hoping that someone - anyone - would hear her over the noise of the train.

Immediately, he jumped up and grabbed her by the throat. She gasped furiously for breath as the train entered the tunnel. By this time he was holding one hand over her mouth. She felt him prodding her in the chest with the knife. She was frozen in fear and totally overpowered.

Suddenly, all the lights went out plunging the whole coach into darkness. Kicking out wildly, she managed to break from his grasp and escape from the compartment. The train was still in the tunnel as she stumbled along the narrow corridor aware that he vas close behind. By chance she found the toilet door, which was open and managed to hide there. Soon, she could hear him trying to open the door and muttering to himself.

If only she could hold out until the train emerged from the tunnel she might be able to call for help and people would be able to see a little with the help of the lights outside. Then she heard a wild scream and the sound of a door banging against the side of the train. The noise of the train indicated that it was clear of the tunnel.

"Had the evil beast jumped or fallen from the train?" she wondered.

She held her breath and slowly opened the toilet door. She was right – the carriage door was open.

Jane was soon grasped by the fear that in some way, perhaps, she was responsible for the man's death. After all, there were no witnesses. How could she prove that he was trying to kill her only minutes before? Her imagination was now starting to run riot. Would a jury believe her story?

The train stopped at the next station and she decided to get off. She would telephone home in the morning and explain she would be arriving later without going into detail. She would try and forget about the whole sordid incident. No doubt the station staff could direct her to a nearby hotel where she could get some sleep and recover before continuing her journey.

As she walked along the wet platform with the rain beating against her face a voice called out:

"Excuse me madam, you've left your holdall behind and your beetroot seems to have spilt."

Sins of the Father

The rain lashed constantly against the windscreen of the taxi as it wound its way through the narrow streets. Joe McCann peered through the steamed up windows straining his eyes as he sought to get his bearing.

"Why did the train have to be late," he thought, "tonight of all nights?"

He could picture Miss Finnerty's face. She would not be very pleased and she was certainly not one to hide her true feelings.

He had rushed home from work to keep the appointment for his daughter's sake. The opportunity to work some overtime had meant him missing the last open evening at the school. The few extra pounds were badly needed and Christmas was not all that far away now.

Miss Finnerty was tall and had a slim graceful figure, which was well preserved for a woman of fifty plus years. She had a domineering personality and a sharp tongue that would cut you to the quick if she felt so inclined. Despite her rather low popularity rating most parents agreed she was a good teacher.

Joe McCann was not really in any position to judge - his eldest daughter Anne was scarcely eight years old. The taxi came to a halt outside the large school gates and he felt his stomach turning at the thought of meeting her. Hopefully, his wife would explain that he worked in London.

'You're late Mr. McCann." said Miss Finnerty, glaring at him over her spectacles.

"I'm sorry Miss Finnerty - the train was late - some problem with the overhead lines due to the bad weather."

She was not interested in his excuses. Yes, as far as she was concerned that's what they were - excuses, not reasons.

The school classroom was bright and welcoming which was more than could be said for Miss Finnerty. He thought about his own village school in Ireland all those years ago. She beckoned him to sit down beside his wife. He felt decidedly awkward and not a little ridiculous sitting on the low child's chair. Miss Finnerty sat on a stool and he felt her large frame bearing down on him.

"I'm not very happy with Anne's progress, Mr. McCann," she said.

"Oh dear," he replied somewhat taken back.

"In fact I will go as far as to say I am disappointed, very disappointed."

There was a noticeable quiver in her bottom lip.

It reminded him of the time he was stopped on the way home from school by Mrs. O'Reilly who was foaming at the mouth and holding the bread knife in her hand. She accused him of making some long forgotten remark about her daughter's knickers.

"She seems to be in a dream most of the time. I haven't got the time to spend with her with 30 other children in the class." continued Miss Finnerty.

Joe McCann had not expected this. Anne was a good little worker who seemed to enjoy school. He felt lost for words. His own schooldays began to flash before his mind. Wasn't he too something of a dreamer?

"Her written work is ... well, the content is fair but the presentation is appalling.

She is much slower than the others in her group."

His wife, who had already heard the bad news, moved uneasily on her chair as she listened. He wondered if teachers were really interested in the slower children - the ones who needed the help. Various examples of her schoolwork were thrust in front of them by Miss Finnerty with little time to study them in any detail.

"She is capable of giving a lot more. Quite honestly, I did wonder of everything was all right at home?" she added.

Joe McCann detected the accusing tone in her voice and resented the inference. He felt his blood pressure starting to rise.

"What did she mean by that remark?" he wondered.

Money was certainly tight even with the odd hour's overtime. The high mortgage rate and rising cost of living meant there was little to spare at the end of the month.

Joe McCann didn't mind admitting that the last six months had been hard. Images of his own impoverished childhood crowded his mind. He was growing angry now. Even a placid man like Joe McCann had his tolerance limits.

"Do you help her at home, Mr. McCann?" she enquired.

Again, she glared at him from over her spectacles.

"Yes...yes, we do try," he answered nervously "the trouble is we're not always sure what is the best way to help her."

He fought to control his feelings - he was finding this increasingly difficult. Things had changed a great deal since his schooldays, he thought. Of course something's never change - Cliff Richard was still in the charts although they don't put his photograph in chewing gum packets any more.

Joe McCann wasn't listening now. Memories of his own schooldays came flooding back through the years and the tears. The words of old Master Gilhooley were echoing in his ears. He could still feel that burning, aching, sensation in his ears after the many belts from the Master's hand.

"Who ever said schooldays were the happiest days of your life?" he asked himself.

Whatever education Joe McCann had received in the primary school had been beaten into him. Old Gilhooley would have done well in the secret police of some East European State. In terms of today's educational system, however, he would be a redundant as an East German border guard.

He could still see him pick up the inkbottle, in a fit of temper, and throw it down the room at him, spattering black ink all over the new copybook in which he struggled to write.

"If only I had not missed so many days at school," he pondered, desperately striving to control the anger that was now welling up inside him.

"You'll never come to anything, McCann." his teacher would say, "Too much time spent gallivanting around the country on that bicycle of yours, that's your trouble."

It wasn't his fault his mother was always ill and he had to cycle four miles to the dispensary and four miles back again. There were other errands too. He had not relished queuing up in the local Garda Station to collect the one-pound supplementary benefit.

125

Then there were all the journeys over the hills to Reagan's to borrow a pound or two when things were really bad. Yes, he knew only too well what was in the carefully sealed envelope. When poverty came in the window shame went out the door.

"Gallivanting" - that's what Gilhooley called it. Like the rest of his clan, he was self-righteous and smug, with little time for the children of the poorer parents - especially the slower children. His mother died shortly after he left school. Damn little good all those white bottles and pills had done for her. There would be no more gallivanting on the bicycle.

Above all, perhaps, it was the favouritism, which the old Master showed which hurt most. It was always the brighter ones who got the praise and the pennies. They could be relied upon to create a favourable impression when the Inspector or the Priest called.

And it was always the same ones who got the job of assisting on special occasions. Like, for example, when the dentist called. Then one of Gilhooley's bright-eyed boys would be given the task of operating that primitive machine which looked like part of a bicycle and powered the drill.

Those were the days before rural electrification. Barbarism by another name, that's what it was. Children wandered around the school playground bleeding and in agony after such visits. It was that peculiar mix of religion, hypocrisy and cruelty, which left its mark on Joe McCann. He accepted that all teachers and schools were not like his - even thirty odd years ago. Still, that was little consolation.

Miss Finnerty's words again echoed in his ears.

"She is much slower than the others in her group..."

Schools and teachers were different now, he thought. He had walked to school in his bare feet in the summer sun with the soft tar squelching between his toes. The winters were hard on young ones. Like so many others, he would walk the two miles through the snow with holes in his Wellingtons and two sods of turf wrapped in newspaper under his arm. Those old classrooms with their tall gable windows and draughty floorboards were cold - bitterly cold. The single black stove in the centre of the room was no match for Jack Frost.

Who would have predicted that this meeting with Miss Finnerty to discuss his own daughter's progress would release a great dam of emotions the like of which he had not felt for years? He was virtually oblivious to Miss Finnerty's words - words now directed to his wife. Anne was being written off at eight years of age just like he had been all those years ago.

Now Miss Finnerty's words had become those of old Master Gilhooley. It was he - Joe McCann - not little Anne, who was being treated as an intellectual failure and thrown onto the educational scrap heap. He felt like exploding inside.

"Damn you, and your school and your educational system!" he screamed.

"Mr.... "

"Don't you Mister me ...you condemn my child as a failure because she does not match up to your standards. Yes, an intellectual and educational failure at eight years."

"Mr. McCann..."

"Yes, just like me, the school dunce - but I made it, yes - despite the schools and the teachers, despite the poverty and the hopelessness, I succeeded."

"But Mr.McCann, listen to..."

"I'm sick listening - listening to voices long dead – voices and images that still haunt me after all those years telling me I'm useless."

"But you must listen, Mr. McCann, for the sake of your child..."

"I love my children and live for my children so that they will not have to endure what I have had to endure, that they will not have to wear the shackles that bind me and so many like me."

The face of old Master Gilhooley was staring at him now. It was clear - ever so clear.

Joe McCann never recalled exactly what had happened. Did the quiet and unassuming father really try and strangle Miss Finnerty? The shouting had stopped now and calm had returned to the little classroom with its tiny chairs and tables. He wiped the tears from his eyes and swallowed hard on the lump, which had formed, in his throat.

Miss Finnerty leaned forward and gently placed her hand on his shoulder.

"It's alright," she said, "I too have my own memories".

He couldn't find any words to answer her.

"But don't you think little Anne will have enough baggage to carry through life without being burdened with yours also?" she said. Their eyes met and he knew only too well what she had meant.

"And as I was trying to explain, Anne just needs a little extra help and encouragement at home and she'll be fine - just fine."

Joe McCann nodded and smiled.

www.ingramcontent.com/pod-product-compliance
Lightning Source LLC
Chambersburg PA
CBHW050307260626
47156CB00005B/1702